Matters of Life and Death

Matters of Life and Death

Lesego Malepe

Writer's Showcase
San Jose New York Lincoln Shanghai

Matters of Life and Death

Writer's Showcase
an imprint of iUniverse.com, Inc.

For information address:
iUniverse.com, Inc.
5220 S 16th, Ste. 200
Lincoln, NE 68512
www.iuniverse.com

ISBN: 0-595-00433-4

Printed in the United States of America

For my parents,

and for my friends Barbara Brown

and David Massey

The Legend-Mamogashwa

A frightening legend lived in Melodi, the black township near Pretoria. Mamogashwa, the snake, hid in the deepest part of the river Moretele where it cut through the Klip mountain that bordered Melodi in the North. Sometimes the snake sunned herself on the surface of the water and then she emerged, not in her true form as a snake, but as a white woman on top and her bottom part, still a snake, submerged. Her long brown silky hair glistened in the sun, and like some said, diamonds sparkled in her hair. She had a beautiful smile and her dreamy eyes gave off an angelic glow.

She liked to feast on children's fresh brains, not tough adult brains, which was why all her victims were young. Parents in Melodi always warned their kids, "Don't play in the river. Mamogashwa will take you. Run when you see a beautiful white woman sitting on the water, even from a distance. Once your eyes meet she will hypnotize you and pull you in. She can also grab you by your shadow."

Every year Mamogashwa drowned at least one child. She would drag the victim to the bottom and suck the child's brains out through the nostrils. Usually she was satisfied with only one brain at a time, so nobody in Melodi forgot the time in nineteen-fifty-nine when she took two children, girls, a rare event since it was boys that often got tricked by her. Girls did not go to the river as much.

White police divers from Pretoria fished their bodies out. It was a good thing that there were no black police divers, because Mamogashwa might have drowned them mercilessly. She would not harm white people of course. So white divers were safe in her part of the river.

Once in a while, Mamogashwa glided through the sky to other parts of the river, miles away. To make sure that nobody saw her she unleashed great fury into the sky, roared as thunder, wrapped herself in thick dark clouds, and pounded the earth below her with heavy rain or furious hail. Her eyes threw sparks of lightning in all directions. She rolled the clouds so they made a deep menacing noise like army tanks that invaded the black townships during uprisings. She belched fire like a dragon, leaving scorched houses, cracked electric poles and split trees. Some educated people erroneously attributed the fires to lightning.

People who dared to look up at the sky and see the light in her eyes were blinded. For most of those who were unfortunate enough to see her, their hearts stopped beating and they died. The few unfortunate souls who saw her but lived could not tell about it anyway, since they lost their minds and their tongues became twisted so they could not talk. The ignorant and uninformed described Mamogashwa's cover as a thunderstorm or tornado, as though it were a natural phenomenon. But the wise ones knew the truth. And, although there was a lot of disagreement about when Mamogashwa came to live there, everyone agreed that she first came with white people.

CHAPTER 1

1963

Thunder roared. There was a knock at the door, the back door.

So late at night in the middle of the week? The back door meant it had to be someone familiar or else a stranger who saw that the lights in the front of the house were off. Edward Maru listened closely. It was not a knock, he thought. The wind must have thrown something against the door. The strange sound almost merged with the thunder, pounding rain and furious winds. It was amazing how rain showers always nourished the earth around Easter—but also very deceiving, because when the weather cleared, cold winter winds settled in. This year though, the rains were unseasonably heavy and rough; it was going to be a tough winter. The cold winds howled outside, but in the kitchen the red coals in the Welcome Dover stove cracked and threw off wild sparks.

Edward continued to grade papers from his Setswana language class at the University of South Africa. His wife Evelyn, who sat at the round table across from him, also graded papers: hers were Standard Four arithmetic exercises. Her red pen moved fast across the pages. Edward wished she had fewer students in her class.

Evelyn looked up at the window for a moment but did not say anything. The rain was wonderful, a blessing, even though cold. Such a shame she had not been able to work in the garden that afternoon. She continued to grade, but at a slower pace.

They were getting used to the deep quiet and extra space in the house, with all four children at boarding school. The three oldest, sons, had been gone for years now, but this was the first year away for their youngest and only surviving girl, thirteen-year-old Neo. They missed her, but each pretended not to feel it as much as the other. Her name meant "gift" in Setswana. Evelyn had decided before Neo was born that they wouldn't have more children, but Edward begged for one more. They might get lucky and get another girl. So when this baby was born she was Neo, a gift, a precious gift. All their children's names meant something related to their birth. Unlike other black children, they did not have Christian or English names. This to Edward, was not a political statement but a matter of pride in his own language and culture, both of which Edward cared about deeply. It was therefore not surprising that he turned out to be the country's leading expert on Setswana, his language.

Edward shook his fountain pen. "Neo would get me another from my bag if she were here…the house is awfully quiet without her."

Evelyn wiped her glasses. "She'd be making tea now. Do you miss her?"

"Oh, no, no. She's just been gone two months," Edward said. "I was just making an observation."

Evelyn smiled and looked him in the eye. "You miss her a little maybe?"

Edward took off his glasses and rubbed his nose. "There's no doubt about it, sending her to boarding school was the best decision. She's sure to get a good education there."

"She's all right," said Evelyn. "She's got her brother with her."

There was a knock, and Evelyn and Edward looked up. The continuous tapping at the door was clear.

"So late at night," Evelyn said, "in this cold rain."

Edward pushed the chair back and went to open the door.

He welcomed his sister Mary's only child. "*Motlogolo*," he exclaimed in Setswana. "My nephew, Ranoka, come in."

Evelyn noticed that their nephew frowned slightly. She knew he preferred to be called by his English name, Peter, but of course his Uncle Edward would not even acknowledge that name. Edward was fond of saying, "White children don't have Setswana names."

Evelyn did not feel strongly one way or another about these naming matters. Peter preferred "Peter" or his nickname "Snakes", which most young people used, but Edward would not call him "Snakes". Edward never ceased to be puzzled by his nephew. "Whoever heard of anybody wishing to be called a snake?" It seemed no coincidence that Peter's surname was Noga. In Setswana, Noga means "snake" and there'd been some unkind comments when Edward's sister married a man with that last name. What kind of name was that? It surprised no one then, that Peter turned out to be untrustworthy, slithery, slippery and shifty. Setswana-speaking people have a proverb: *leina lebe seromo*. People tend to live up to their names.

Edward offered Peter his own chair, facing the front of the stove. "Sit down and warm yourself. It's cold out tonight. You look like you've seen a ghost."

Peter coughed with a shallow cough, the type used to clear a space before a verbal bomb is dropped. He hit at his chest. "Just irritated."

"Move closer to the fire," Evelyn said. "You could catch a nasty cold in this weather. You know, there's a bad strain of flu coming this year. Hong Kong flu or something."

Peter pressed his throat like a doctor feeling for swollen glands. "Just irritated from talking too much today. Heavy teaching day, meetings. Teaching really is a job."

"As you can see, we are also at it, grading." Evelyn said, "How are the children? Are they all right?"

Peter rubbed his hands together. "The children are fine, Auntie."

"They are such a joy at that age," Evelyn said. "Just feed them, give them a little hug there, and it's all done."

Edward poked the fire through the small horizontal bars on the little stove door. "It is very important to spend time with them. They grow quickly. Is their mother well?"

"She's fine too, *Malome*," Peter said, using the Setswana word for uncle. "There is no problem." He took off his felt hat, whch was an expensive gray Dobbs, and held it between his hands. "Oh, sorry Auntie, I forget I'm wearing a hat."

"It's this rain," Evelyn said. "They say it's raining in the whole country. I hope it's not flooding in Natal like last year, leaving all those poor people stranded without houses. We are lucky up here."

As she spoke, Peter took off the plastic rain shoes he wore over his shiny black American Florsheims.

As Evelyn watched her nephew, she wondered if he had come to borrow money from them. He had seemed to have stopped borrowing for quite some time, to every relative's relief. He still acted like a boy, spending a lot of his money on expensive clothes and shoes, but Evelyn liked him better these days. He seemed to be maturing and finally behaving like a grown, married man. It was hard though, to understand how he maintained such a high life-style.

"You can put your hat here," Edward said.

"No, it's all right, *Malome*." Peter kept his hat in his hands and shook it nervously. "I have some bad news."

Evelyn sat upright. "Bad news?" She and Edward looked at each other.

Peter pushed his chair back and sat ramrod stiff as though that would straighten his story. "The police arrested some boys tonight at school in Hebron. Tiro has been picked up too. Boy stuff, you know."

Evelyn sighed. "Arrested?"

"Was there a strike?" Edward asked.

Peter tapped his knee. "We are not sure what happened. Maybe they were plotting a strike. You know the authorities don't ignore these strikes anymore. These white principals are like policemen."

Thunder grumbled outside. Evelyn felt as if a spark went through her body. Boys usually get into trouble. But at least her family had been lucky. There were many boys in the family but few problems so far. Good upbringing made a difference.

Edward took his glasses off. "What happened?"

Peter's hands trembled and the hat trembled in them, shaking as though moved by an earth tremor. "Nobody knows."

Evelyn folded her books in a neat pile and rose from her chair. Her forehead was creased and her eyes were narrowed as if she could see better if she squeezed her eyes. She held one hand on her slim waist. "You mean even the teachers don't know anything?"

Peter scratched his forehead. "You know how the Special Branch is."

"The Special Branch!" Edward said.

Evelyn raised her voice. "What does the Special Branch have to do with school children? Oh my God."

"Since when has the Special Branch involved itself in school matters?" Edward asked. "Even during the worst school strikes, the Special Branch didn't intervene; the regular police did. Are you sure it was the Special Branch?"

Peter nodded and stared at his shiny shoes.

"Tiro's not the type to get into trouble," Evelyn said, more to herself than to the others. She found it hard to believe this news about her third son. "He's always been quiet and he's never given us any trouble."

"It's probably nothing," Peter said.

Edward stroked the big bald spot on the top of his head. "How many boys were arrested?"

"Four," Peter said. "Some of the students the special Branch were looking for could not be found. Those students must have suspected something."

Peter got up and rested one hand on the back of the chair. "Sorry, I have to go. I have an early morning class tomorrow, and since I'm sleeping at home tonight, it means I have to get up extra early tomorrow."

"You are smart to rent a room at Hebron and sleep there some nights. Otherwise, the commute would kill you," Evelyn said. "Anyway, thank you very much for taking the trouble to drive through this stormy rain to tell us."

Peter picked up his rain shoes. "Don't have to wear these. I'm going straight home."

Edward and Evelyn walked him to the door. Peter had parked right in front of the kitchen door. They stood at the covered stoop as Peter got into his car and drove away.

Edward shook his head. "Look at him. He told us he was going straight home, but he's going in the opposite direction, God knows where."

"He can come through in unexpected ways sometimes," Evelyn said, trying to be fair. "I think he's maturing these days. In the past, he would have waited a day to come here. He wouldn't have braved this weather."

They remained standing on the stoop. Evelyn wrapped her arms around her body. "It's so cold. When it clears we'll find that winter has arrived. It always comes in under the cover of rain."

They went back inside and locked the door.

Edward picked up his glasses from the table. "I think I need new glasses. These are weak now."

Evelyn held her hands to her waist. "I can't understand all of this."

Edward slumped against the cupboard and wiped his glasses with his handkerchief. He blew onto them and wiped some more. "Boys are always getting into trouble. It's probably something about organizing a strike, maybe…"

Evelyn cupped her jaw in her right hand. "I can't believe this."

Edward let out a deep sigh. "I hope they don't get expelled. Then, I'll have to go to the Melodi High School principal again, and put the poor man in a difficult position once more."

"At least we're lucky he's our friend." Evelyn said. "Besides, we are not the only ones asking for this kind of favor. People do it all the time."

Edward stroked his bald spot and looked down. "The things children will make you do."

He went to the stove and with the poker turned the coals so the fire crackled with fresh flames and new vigor.

"Children are so unpredictable," Evelyn said.

Edward retrieved his pipe from the ashtray in the dining room, then sat down in the kitchen and filled his pipe. "Peer pressure is very strong at this stage," he said without looking up. "You know, Tiro's quiet so he sometimes has to prove that he is not a coward."

Evelyn was in no mood for these psychological explanations. Edward always had neat reasonable justifications for things. Edward's college majors had been psychology and Setswana. Evelyn remembered when Edward taught child psychology at Kilnerton Teacher Training College. But language was always his passion; it was not surprising that he ended up teaching Setswana in the department of African languages at the University of South Africa.

Slowly they cleaneed up the kitchen, turned out the lights throughout the house, then retired to the bedroom. In bed, Evelyn and Edward asked each other the same questions. Was it a strike? Was it about the loss of Kilnerton? For hours they talked, unable to sleep. At last, each lay dead quiet pretending to sleep so that the other could sleep. Outside the wind howled and the rain pounded the gutters. Evelyn prayed silently.

Chapter 2

Looking For Tiro

Edward and Evelyn both got up early the next morning, at four instead of the usual five o'clock. After a night of tossing and turning into endless sleeping positions and staring at the clock, with Edward getting up to drink water and Evelyn looking through the window to see if it was still raining, they awoke as tired as they were the night before.

Evelyn went to the window, pulled back the thick beige curtains, and looked outside. "The clouds are still dense. I think the worst is yet to come."

Edward turned to face the window. "It can't rain much longer. The ground is soaked. But I guess people at home need it, since last year's harvest was not so good." Edward was referring to Fafung, where he grew up and where his ailing mother still lived. He had not lived there since he was sixteen. Since the one-room school at Fafung went only up to Standard Five, he'd left to go to school about thirty miles away in Jericho.

Edward watched as Evelyn returned to bed and he was glad about the rain. Now, she wouldn't have to water the garden before going to school. He had tried to persuade her many times to get someone to help her, but she always declined, saying it would be an unnecessary waste of money. He used to feel guilty about not helping her much in the garden, but then got used to it. Anyway, on the few occasions he tried to help she'd said he messed things up and couldn't tell the difference between weeds and good plants. They used to laugh about it since he was the one who had worked hard in the fields as a child. Maybe that's why gardening couldn't be a hobby for him. Evelyn really enjoyed working in the garden. She was an amazing woman, headstrong too and once she made up her mind there was no moving her.

"So many strikes in high schools," Edward said, more to himself than to Evelyn.

Evelyn said, "A black principal usually is not quick to press charges, but a white principal is always ready to destroy black children."

Without information on what led to Tiro's arrest, they settled on strikes as the reason. They simply refused to consider anything more serious. Tiro was the quietest of their children, not a joiner, more a loner. They knew their children.

"I'd be worried if it were Pitso," Edward said. "He's capable of anything, he's stubborn, a fighter."

"Tiro really is our easiest child," Evelyn said.

"Also a good student," Edward continued. "Very hard-working, he'll go very far."

They listened silently to the whistling wind for a while. It would be nice if this was a Saturday, Edward mused, so they could sleep in a bit. But, thank God, it wasn't because then they'd have had to wait the whole weekend to find out about poor Tiro. Not much happened in government matters on weekends.

"At least we should be grateful this happens early in the year and not at the end towards exam time," Evelyn said. "I'm glad he'll be done with high school this year."

Edward swung around and sat on the edge of the bed. "You're right. The boys can make up for lost time and be settled by the time exam time comes. Maybe they'll lose about a month, which isn't too bad."

"I hope they don't get suspended."

"Then, he'll have to write final Matric exams as a private candidate," Edward said.

"I wish we could go to see him together," Evelyn said, "but the school inspector is coming to my class today."

"I'll go," Edward said. "It's all right." He paused, then continued, "Would you like me to pick you up after school? We can go and see him then."

She sighed deeply. "These inspections are a pain sometimes, but it will be fine."

"Should I pick you up after two then?" Edward asked.

"No, you go ahead and see him," Evelyn said.

"Since it's Friday, if he isn't released today, you may not see him until Monday."

They went out to the kitchen.

In the kitchen Evelyn opened the door and inhaled the fresh air deeply. It smelled of the wet earth. She stood on the back stoop and Edward joined her. The rain fell harder.

Edward wasn't in a hurry; on rainy days he left much later so he could take Evelyn to school. He particularly didn't mind that day because he could only go to Central after nine; that was when government offices usually opened.

Evelyn left Edward standing on the stoop and went inside. Minutes later she came out wearing her work rain-coat, a man's heavy bright yellow plastic one. She took the keys for the shed and marched into her garden.

"Evelyn, you can't go out in the pouring rain," Edward said, shaking his head. "All we need is for you to catch a cold."

"I don't get colds. You are the one who always gets colds. Besides, working with flowers in the rain isn't bad. This is the perfect time to work with the soil."

She adjusted the rain hat. "I won't stay out long. I'll just weed around the roses."

Edward stood on the stoop, lost in thought. After a few minutes he went back into the kitchen.

Evelyn followed.

"Ed," she began, "that tree in front looks like it has been hit by lightning."

"Fallen limbs?" he asked.

"No, a crack down the stem."

They both went out to look. The tree looked severely damaged. Their eyes met though neither spoke, not a good luck sign.

Later, Edward dropped Evelyn off at her school and drove towards Pretoria. The rain was still falling hard and he liked the drumming on the roof of the car and the rhythmic sound of the windshield wipers. This steady beat calmed him, the sound of rubber against glass soothed him.

He drove through Silverton, past the former Kilnerton High School, his alma mater. The buildings hadn't been demolished yet. How sad it was that Kilnerton had not lasted long enough for all his children to graduate there. Just one more year, and Tiro would have graduated. Instead, he had to go to Hebron for his final year. That's the the way white people toyed with black lives.

The rain finally stopped, but the sky looked like the clouds were just resting, gone to draw more water to pound the earth again. The rain was a blessing. God knows after the past year's drought they needed it, but sometimes it was not good. He hoped the night's lightning hadn't struck any people or houses.

Edward was soon on Pretorius street. He hit the brakes, his heart beating rapidly. He didn't want to get a speeding ticket. Strange how he didn't feel the speed, sixty-five miles per hour. These wide one-ways lulled him into forgetting he was in town.

He parked the car at the University of South Africa where he worked. It was easier and cheaper than struggling with parking meters or garages in the center of town.

He walked slowly towards Central Police Station a few blocks away. He'd never been in there before. He felt queasy. It would've been better if he'd eaten his usual breakfast; not good to disturb the body's routines. His head felt heavy, not a real headache, but a dull droning in his skull.

He stood before the dark brick building and took a deep breath. He adjusted his gray jacket and climbed the gray stairs that seemed unending. At the top, he went toward with the sign that read "nie-blanke/non-white."

A black officer in a stiff dark khaki uniform approached.

"What are you looking for? Can I help you?" The officer asked.

Edward was surprised by this politeness. The officer was not extra courteous. It was just that Edward expected the worst in a place like this. Who ever heard of a decent police-man in Central? Especially, considering that there was a white policeman nearby. He knew from experience that black officers were usually normal when no white people were around, but as soon as their white superiors appeared, they were rude. It was part of the job. The black officer did-n't exactly smile, but the corners of his mouth were soft, raised ever so slightly.

"I'm looking for my son, I'm told he is detained here," Edward said.

The black officer creased his brow, bit his lower lip and pointed to a white policeman on the phone behind the counter. "Sit by the bench and wait for him."

Edward sat on the dark brown bench against the dark brown wall. Police wandered in and out. Some of them were in plain clothes, and Edward knew they were probably security police. The thought made Edward's brow hot. He pulled out his handkerchief, removed his glasses and wiped his face, He then wiped his hands too. There was not enough air in the room. He took a deep breath.

The white officer hung up the phone. The black officer went to him to tell him about Edward, but the officer raised his hand, stopping him; then he made another call.

Edward stood and began to speak to the black officer. "My son is one of the Kilnerton boys the police…" Before he could finish, the policeman raised his hand and shook his head. "We are not allowed to answer any inquiries."

It all sounded complicated. Edward returned to the bench. What could he expect? Everything to do with the government was becoming more bureaucratic and more involved. When Edward applied for his passport renewal, he was surprised at the extra information he had to furnish. The red tape was growing unnecessarily complicated.

The white officer finally put the phone down, and Edward watched as the other officer whispered to him.

Edward got up when the white police officer approached him. The officer asked in Afrikaans "When was he detained?" All this was said rapidly and in the usual barking tone that the police and government officials often used with Africans.

Edward answered as best he could.

Then the officer disappeared into the back and returned with an older white policeman.

"Well," the older white officer said, "Yes, they were arrested."

Edward hesitated before he finally asked, "Can I see him?"

"They were detained under the Ninety-Day Detention clause," the officer said. "So you can't see him."

The ground seemed to sway and Edward steadied himself by gripping the edge of the counter. It dawned on Edward that this was a political arrest. Tiro...A seventeen year old detained under the ninety-day act? Yes he'd heard of detentions under this law; it was all over the English papers, which he read. Maybe the officer didn't understand.

"The students from Hebron High School," Edward said speaking slowly. "You sure there's no mistake."

"We don't make mistakes here, *monna*," the officer said in Afrikaans.

Edward swallowed hard. The reference to him as 'monna' rankled, and he felt humiliated, but what could he do? The Government had decided that in dealings with black men, white government officials should not address them as Meneer(the Afrikaans equivalent of Mister) since that put them on the same plane as white men. White government officials would address black men as '*Monna*'. Black men found this offensive.

But it was silly since the word "*monna*" actually meant "man" in Edward's language.

Like most educated Africans, Edward's Afrikaans was nowhere as good as his English, but he spoke it correctly-text-book Afrikaans. It was the language of torture, of humiliation. Even for someone who was passionate about languages as he was, Afrikaans was to be only endured, not enjoyed.

"Are they held here?" Edward asked.

"We can't say…, maybe, maybe not," the white officer said and walked away.

Edward looked at the black officer who dropped his eyes then bent to tie his big brown round-nosed shoes. Edward sighed, not wanting to put him in a tight spot with his white superiors.

Edward walked down the stairs slowly. His legs felt heavy like he was wearing iron shackles. When he reached the bottom, he kept his gaze down. People rushed around him, but he needed to think. His son, Tiro, a detainee?

The Ninety-Day Detention Act was for serious political offenses, crimes adults committed. How could teens, children in a boarding school, seriously threaten the state? Obviously some mistake…the whole thing would clear up soon.

Edward stepped outside. It was colder than the morning even though the rain had stopped.

He thought of calling Evelyn, but remembered the school's phone was in the principal's office. The principal would have to call her; so he decided against it.

He went to his office. He closed the door and sat at his desk and smoked his pipe. Instead of just letting it hang in his mouth the way he usually did, he inhaled deeply. He was in a daze, but he knew he had to consult a lawyer.

After a while he looked up the lawyer's number. He called and to his surprise, he got an appointment to see him that afternoon.

Edward met with the lawyer, Mr. Gous, a friendly older white man. Edward explained Tiro's predicament to him.

"The police did not say anything?" Mr. Gous asked. "The school?"

"They said they didn't know, but the boys were taken by the Security Police."

"Security police?" Mr. Gous asked. "How old is he?"

"He'll be eighteen in August."

"Mmm," Mr. Gous tapped his pen on the table and looked out the window, then back at Edward. "If he was picked up by the Security Police then it's a more serious matter."

He called in his secretary and told her to phone around to see where Tiro Maru was being held. She came back in a few minutes with no information.

"I'll have to go to Central to look for him," Mr. Gous said, sighing "It's better to go in person."

Edward and the lawyer walked to Central.

Mr. Gous spoke Afrikaans to the officer who came out to see them. They chatted for a while, while Edward sat on the bench. Mr. Gous asked Edward to wait and he disappeared into a back office with a plainclothes officer. He returned after a few minutes, frowning, and he and Edward stepped outside. The rain had stopped but the clouds hovered, thick, menacing. It looked as though the sky was closing in and the clouds would explode and drown the earth in a tidal wave.

"Mr. Maru," Mr. Gous said softly "It looks like we may have a serious problem. But, they are high school students so it may not be too bad, I'd really worry if these were university students."

"Is Tiro here?" Edward asked. "Can I see him?"

"Yes, eh, let's hope. But you can't see him, now," Mr. Gous said. "Sorry."

Edward removed his glasses and polished them with his handkerchief. He rubbed the sides of his nose where the glasses pressed.

"Can *you* see him?" Edward asked.

"Nobody can see him. The police can hold him without charging him for ninety days. And in that time, the detainees have no access to anybody, not even lawyers."

"Are they being tortured?" Edward asked. "My son so young…"

"Let's hope for the best," Mr. Gous said. "They were in school, so they couldn't have done anything too serious."

Everybody knew the Detention Act was passed so the police could torture the detainees during interrogations and have enough time to let them heal before they appeared in court or before they could be seen by their lawyers and families.

He remembered the rumors he heard about what they did to political detainees, electric shocks in sensitive parts of the body, immersion in cold water, keeping them awake for days, beatings with all kinds of objects. Edward couldn't bear to think about this. He said a silent prayer for God to protect his child.

"Mr. Maru," Edward heard a voice that seemed far away, as though muffled by clouds. "Are you all right?"

Edward was startled. "No, I was just thinking."

His son is a "detainee". Sounded worse than "prisoner." He remembered the flurry of security legislation, and the endless amendments. He thought things were getting bad, but his children weren't very active. The police were probably just politicizing everything. Since the nineteen-sixty Sharpeville protests, even students who complained about bad food in boarding school were labeled "political". These Afrikaners were really going crazy arresting eighteen year old kids.

Edward walked back to his office, got into his car and drove home. It wasn't raining, but the clouds, darker now, hung low and ominous in the sky.

When he arrived home, Evelyn was already there. "So how did it go?" she asked anxiously. "How is he?"

"It looks a little more serious than we thought," Edward said.

Evelyn rested her elbows on the table and cupped her face in her hands.

"What do you mean serious?" she asked.

He took his glasses off and rubbed his eyes a bit, and then explained the day's events.

"What do the security police have to do with school problems?" Evelyn asked.

"It's politics, Gous said." Edward explained. "Detention under the ninety-day Clause is only for political cases, so it's a political case."

"What political case?" Evelyn pressed. "Tiro's not active. The soccer team is the only thing he joined."

"The lawyer will try to find out more, but it's difficult. The police aren't required to give any information or to press charges until after ninety days."

"What!" Evelyn said. "These Boers are going after our children now?"

"If it's not serious," Edward began, "they might just be released soon, without their being charged. Maybe it's just some small thing and they are trying to scare these boys".

Evelyn was shocked at this charge of political involvement. Edward didn't belong to any organization. A quiet
and private man, he kept a low profile even in church affairs.
Evelyn remembered being surprised at the Commissioner's
Office when they registered the birth of their first son, Pitso.
The white official asked for a Christian name for the child
and Edward said firmly, "My children are Setswana-speaking and there is no reason why they should carry foreign
names." So, their kids didn't have Christian names to be
used for official purposes. That was Edward's most flagrant
political act. It had more to do with his passion for language
than with politics. But it came to be perceived as a political
act anyway. She loved their names and each had a special
meaning: their first, Pitso, meant a call, it was the beginning.
Their second child Kagiso, born during the war meant
peace, a prayer for peace. Their third, Tiro meant work.
Evelyn had continued to work to the day Tiro was born. And
their fourth who had died accidentally four years before,
was named Dikeledi, which meant 'tears', because she was
born the day Edward's father died. Then later came their
baby, the child they decided would be last, Neo. The final gift
of all. Evelyn thought about how uncanny it was that her
children lived up to their names.

"Something is wrong here," Evelyn said suddenly. Tiro is
the most hard-working kid. Give him a task, and he keeps at
it until it's done."

"I never thought about it," Edward said, "but you know the saying, *leina lebe seromo*," he said referring to the Setswana phrase that people lived up to their names.

Evelyn felt a sharp pain in her heart. Their eyes met but they each averted their gaze. Evelyn suspected Edward was thinking the same thing: Dikeledi, whose name meant "tears", died young, bringing tears that no longer fell outside on the cheeks but continued to fall inside with each heartbeat. Pitso lived up to his name, heeding calls to action. He had been president of the youth club and was active in various groups. Kagiso was the most peaceful of his children, always a peacemaker. Neo was cheerful, loving and got along with everybody, and she was charming so everybody loved her. Edward adored her.

Edward and Evelyn slept little that night.

Edward called the lawyer the next morning. Nothing new. The newspapers carried the story of detentions in other areas, but not their area. The minister of justice was quoted as saying, "Outside forces together with some organizations in the country are trying to destabilize the country and overthrow the government. This is all part of a world-wide Communist onslaught." He vowed the government would protect "our way of life" and would deal firmly with the agitators. The principal of the local high school, Mr. Metsi, disappeared; the police were looking for him. It was rumored that he had fled to Botswana. Edward was surprised because Mr. Metsi was not known to belong to any political organization.

That night as they again lay sleepless, they listened to the gurgling of rain through the gutters. Then, the rain stopped, and it was quiet for a while. The dog next door barked and on the other side of the house, cats fought and screeched. A car slowed and then drove off. They drifted in and out of sleep. The coming of dawn was a relief. This crisis was new for them.

"Should we tell the children?" Edward asked.

"Maybe we can wait a bit," Evelyn said, "I'd tell Pitso and Kagiso, but Neo, I'm not sure. It's her first year away from home, so maybe we should wait."

"We can't tell Kagiso and not Neo when they're in the same school," Edward said. "Let's wait a bit and see, maybe we are just making a big deal out of a small problem."

Evelyn was not convinced, but remained silent.

A week passed. Edward and Evelyn's conversations were brave attempts to believe this imprisonment would pass without too much harm. The rain came and went with the new season. Evelyn worked harder in the garden after school. She got up early and watered in the morning too.

It was a relief for Edward to immerse himself in the details of his academic office work. He went in early, as always, and with difficulty kept to his routines as if nothing was bothering him.

Evelyn convinced Edward that he should go ahead with his trip to Botswana, since it seemed nothing would be done anyway. His passport was in order and he had already made all the arrangements. Postponing the trip would mess up his schedule.

He was reluctant, but Evelyn pressed him to go. "It's only a six-hour drive, you can come home if you need to," she reminded him.

CHAPTER 3

Saturday

A week later, on Saturday morning, Evelyn got up early, and as usual made tea. She took a cup to Edward, placing it on the side table next to him. He mumbled a thank you and turned over, repeating the thank you in a louder voice. It always amazed her how this little act made him happy. She did it every morning, and every morning he was grateful. He was the kind of man who never asked anyone to make him tea once he was up, but he appreciated having the first cup in bed. She did not mind doing this for him. Unlike other men, he did a lot of things for himself. She herself did not like lingering in bed and she got up as soon as she awakened.

She took her tea cup outside and stood on the stoop, sipping it. There was a thin sharp wind. She went inside, finished her tea and went to work in the garden.

She weeded around the roses in front. She was surprised at the yellow rose bush, her favorite, which had many flowers on it. Two big ones were open. She touched them gently so as not to crush them, but also to avoid being stung by the thorns. She decided she was going to leave them on the bush. She pulled the dead carnations. She weeded around the yellow marigolds that bordered the fence. These were great because they could stand up to the cold-survivors.

Thirty minutes later Edward took a cup of tea to where Evelyn was working in the garden. She thanked him and paused to drink.

"I think I'll go to the office for a while," he said. "Won't stay too long. Just sort things out a bit. It's quiet so I'll be able to catch up, do a few things."

Edward left for the University and Evelyn continued her gardening.

Moments after Edward left, Evelyn looked up and saw her mother approaching from down the street. She walked briskly for a woman in her seventies. Her visits were more frequent these days because she was worried about Tiro. Evelyn knew she was going to ask questions and she worked out a way to phrase the answers carefully so as not to alarm Koko. Koko meant 'grandmother' and Evelyn started calling her mother Koko when her first child was born. Since then, everybody called Evelyn's mother Koko. The practice was common. The same thing with her children's friends in the neighborhood; they called her "Mummy" which is what her children called her.

Koko was tall, taller than Evelyn who herself was taller than her husband. Her face was smooth, with only a few wrinkles around the eyes.

"Anything new about Tiro?" Koko asked.

"No, they still won't allow anybody to see him, not even lawyers." She explained, "but time goes by fast; they'll be out soon."

Koko adjusted the blue print scarf tied around her head, revealing some white hair. She always wore something on her head when she was out of the house. Koko stood with her arms folded over her chest.

Marie, a young woman who attended Tiro's school greeted them with her usual smile.

"Marie, you home for the weekend?" Koko said.

"Yes, Koko," Marie said.

"How are things at school?" Evelyn asked. "Have you students heard why the boys were arrested?"

Marie looked down. "No, Auntie. Nobody knows what is happening, and they aren't saying anything. Even the teachers say they don't know anything. And, the principal doesn't tell them anything either."

"A strike maybe," Evelyn said.

"The other boys say there were no protest rumors." Marie said softly. "I have to run, Auntie. Mama is waiting for the butter. She's baking today."

"That's okay," Evelyn said.

"Marie, you seem to have stretched out a lot of inches since you went to Hebron," Koko said.

Marie chuckled and walked towards the direction of the stores.

"What a lovely young woman," Koko said.

"Maybe your oldest grandson will marry her one day." Evelyn said, "Who knows?"

This was good news for Koko. They'd seen Marie grow up before their eyes. "Pitso? Really? That's just a wish, or you've seen something?" Koko asked.

"I think there's something between them," Evelyn said. "We saw the amorous looks between them during the holidays last time."

"Would be nice if they married people from Kilnerton and not these people we don't know," Koko said.

They went inside and Evelyn poured a cup of tea for her mother. Koko wore a deep blue print apron that wrapped around her waist.

Evelyn tugged her mother's apron. "Ma, you still wearing that patched apron? People will think you don't have good clothes, and they'll think we don't look after you."

Koko looked at her apron and smoothed it in front. "It's still good, patched neatly, I can't throw away something that's still useful. Would be a waste."

Evelyn shook her head. "You can give it to someone."

"It's too old to give to someone."

"What are you saving all your good aprons and clothes for?"

"So you can use them when I'm dead," Koko said.

"We buy them for you to use," Evelyn said, laughing and shaking her head.

Marie's mother, Dolly came to visit Evelyn.

"Eve, what is this we hear about the children being detained?" Dolly asked.

"Nobody knows what's going on," Evelyn said. "It's all crazy, hope it will all get sorted out soon."

Evelyn told her about the week's events.

It wasn't surprising that Dolly was the first neighbor to check in. They all came from Kilnerton village, where they'd been forcibly removed nine years earlier in nineteen-fifty-four to make room for whites. They had all fought the forced removal together. It was always the Marus that Marie ran to when her father beat her mother, usually on Saturday nights when Fred was drunk. One day, Evelyn shook Fred and hurled him against the sofa. She told him she'd give him a good beating if he ever hurt his wife again. Her threat was credible, since as a girl growing up in Kilnerton, she had beaten up a boy for spreading rumors about her. For some months, Dolly's husband didn't beat her.

The story was a favorite joke around the neighborhood. Even the ministers heard about it and told Evelyn that it wasn't a good thing to use violence to remedy violence. But Evelyn was never repentant. Actually, after threatening Dolly's husband that night, she had scolded Dolly and said,

"You can beat him up. Look at him, so drunk, he can't even stand straight." Fred and Evelyn, childhood friends, eventually patched things up.

The depth of Evelyn and Dolly's bond though, came from another incident, four years before, which linked them together for life.

It happened on a Sunday afternoon after church. Both the Marus and Selomas had been to service that morning and Evelyn walked back home with Dolly. They talked about the goings on in the Manyano, the womens' organization of their church. When they parted they promised to continue the conversation sometime.

When Evelyn got home she found her boys already busy setting the table and preparing for dinner. After dinner they cleaned up. She never forgot how growing up as an only girl among four boys in her family, she'd always borne a heavier load of the housework. She'd vowed to make sure her daughters did not suffer the same fate. She made sure her children worked hard around the house; she didn't bargain with them. The only thing they weren't required to do was gardening; Tiro was the one who volunteered to do that regularly. Evelyn always said the worst thing you could do to your children was spoil them. The world was hard out there, and they won't survive if they're lazy. "What would happen to them if we died?" she'd often say to Edward. Nobody would want to take care of spoiled orphans, but if they are hardworking, she reasoned, relatives will fight to keep them. Nobody wants spoiled brats.

Evelyn's children, especially the girls knew they had to tell where they were going if it was beyond their street. Her older daughter, Dikeledi, and Marie had been close friends since childhood. They were baptized the same day, in the same church in Kilnerton by the same minister. Marie came to get Dikeledi. They told Evelyn they were going to the Kholi street to play with the girls there. It was common to refer to streets by the names of the people who lived there since like most black townships, the streets had no names. That kind of stuff was for white suburbs. The township was divided into sections and the houses had numbers that were not duplicated. The Kilnerton people tended to stick together even in Melodi so Evelyn said okay since she knew the parents well.

Dikeledi and her girl friends, all of them around fourteen, had secretly plotted to walk to the deep part of the river Moretele where Mamogashwa lived. Evelyn heard Dikeledi tell Neo not to follow her. When Evelyn tried to persuade Dikeledi to let Neo go, Dikeledi suggested that Neo should go play with her own friends. Evelyn couldn't understand this since they were girls that Neo knew well in that street. Evelyn solved the problem by saying Dikeledi could go alone, and then later Neo would go by herself. That way Neo wouldn't crowd her older sister. Evelyn realized girls were quite strange in their teen years. Dikeledi was a good girl, so Evelyn wasn't worried. Neo was a good kid too but she often bothered Dikeledi.

Neo didn't see Dikeledi as the young woman she thought she was. Neo protested when Dikeledi left hurriedly.

Neo followed after about thirty minutes. But when she got to the round street with a play field in the middle, she heard from her friends that Dikeledi and several other older girls had gone to the Moretele river. They swore Neo to secrecy because the girls would get punished if the adults found out. Neo, still mad with Dikeledi, thought about running home and telling her mother, knowing Dikeledi would surely get punished, or worse, her mother would go to the river and drag her back home which would embarrass Dikeledi.

Neo was tempted to go to the river but she remembered her mother's words, "I'll kill you myself if you ever set foot in the river." She did not wish to take the risk.

Nine girls went to the river together that Sunday afternoon. When they got to the river they were surprised to find no boys. At first, they sat about ten feet away from the bank of the river. They hoped to see Mamogashwa. Sindi suggested they throw little rocks to wake her, since she was probably sleeping. But, when Sindi stepped forward, Dikeledi pulled her back. "Don't go near," she said, "remember once she gets hold of your shadow, she pulls you in and then you're gone forever."

Martha said, "Remember the boys last year? Mamogashwa pulled Moss in by his shadow."

Sindi stepped forward and Dikeledi pulled her back. They stopped struggling and Sindi said, "I'm joking. I wouldn't dare go near."

Dikeledi said, "You want to get us into trouble, we shouldn't be here in the first place. My mother will kill me if she finds out."

"Your mother is strict, even at school her class is always quiet."

Gladys asked, "Is she as tough at home?"

Dikeledi said, "No." But, she remembered how her older brothers always told her and Neo how lucky they were to have come later when their mother was tired of being strict.

Dikeledi looked at the water. "My grandmother says it's all superstitions, witchcraft stuff. There's no Mamogashwa. It's just a story people tell to scare children. Tornadoes aren't caused by the snake-woman. They're natural, God's things."

The girls crept nearer and sat on the bank of the river. Sindi sat on a rock overhanging the river. Suddenly Sindi slipped, fell in and screamed, "help" while flailing about. The girls screamed with her. Dikeledi raced forward and jumped in to rescue Sindi but soon both were swept under. The girls cried and pulled Martha who also tried to jump in to save them. Leaving their friends in the water, the other girls ran the half mile to the nearest home and called for help. Neighborhood people ran to the river and stood around crying and whispering, "Mamogashwa did it again."

The black police from the local station came and stood around asking questions. Not much they could do since diving and water rescue training were reserved for whites only.

The women wailed, "The government should drain this bloody river before it finishes our children!" Women wept; men stood around feeling helpless and ashamed they couldn't do anything.

After forty minutes the white police came. They dove under to look for the kids.

Two young boys ran to the Maru house. "They've drowned, they've drowned," the taller boy said.

Evelyn tried to calm them down. "Who drowned?"

"Dikeledi and Marie."

It was as though she was in some dream suddenly.

"Where?"

"At the river, at the mountain. Mamogashwa took them."

Evelyn froze. The river had taken lives before but she was sure the boys were wrong...

The two girls had been baptized together, and now were buried together at the cemetry.

Evelyn never stopped blaming herself for not sensing that Dikeledi was up to something. From that point on, she had vowed to watch her children closely to see if they were hiding dangerous plans. She played the scene over and over in her mind. Dikeledi had looked too anxious about dumping Neo that day; she should have known something was wrong.

The Methodist Church Congregation of Melodi was devastated by the tragedy. For months there was some uneasiness between the two mothers. But as time passed they got closer, never talking about the drowning incident, though. They shared a bond which everybody agreed was special and very sad.

Meanwhile, newspapers, radio, and word of mouth spread the news of Tiro's arrest so neighbors, colleagues, acquaintances, and friends stopped by the Maru household to express their concern. A lot of them hoped to learn something definite from the Marus and were disappointed to learn that they too were in the dark as to what was happening.

Evelyn and Koko sat in the kitchen listening to the news.

On the state-owned radio, the Minister of Justice, Mr. Kamp, nicknamed the "bulldog", issued the usual threat about crushing all those who would try to overthrow the state.

They heard the gate creek. Peter drove in and parked in front of the garage. He walked into the house and went straight to the fruit bowl on the kitchen table and he took a big red apple and bit it with a loud smack.

Evelyn and Koko exchanged glances and Evelyn rolled her eyes.

Peter said, "How are you Koko, *Ma-malome*?" His mouth was full of the apple he was chewing.

"We are fine." Koko said.

"Have you heard anything through the grapevine?" Evelyn asked.

Peter leaned against the cupboard. "No, Koko, nothing"

Koko massaged the callus on her hand.

"Sit down, Peter. You're sapping us of blood. "And, you're too heavy on our shoulders," Koko said referring to their belief that a person standing over others did this.

Peter dragged the chair out roughly and it screeched on the blue tiles. He sat sideways on the edge and crossed his legs.

Evelyn told him of Edward's experiences trying to see Tiro.

Peter shifted on his chair and uncrossed his legs and edged closer to the table.

"Don't worry, Auntie. All this will blow over."

"Have you heard any rumors, anything at all?" Evelyn asked.

"No, the principal is not saying a word," Peter said. "I thought maybe he told the white teachers, but when I asked Mr. Oosthuizen, he said they hadn't heard a thing."

"Keep your ears open," Evelyn said. "At least you're on good terms with these white folks. You have a way with them."

Peter tapped his knee and smiled. "Ah, the Boers are like children," he said. "You just have to know how to handle them. Otherwise, they can get vicious and upset. They are never going to go away…"

"Sounds like poisonous snakes to me," Evelyn said.

"They are the rulers," Peter said. "What can we say? And, the way things look, they are here to stay and I guess we have to do the best with the situation."

Koko waved her finger in the air. "Ah, ah, ah, you never know. Remember the old saying, everything comes to an end sometime—and that which does not come to an end, would be a miracle."

Evelyn drummed her finger on the table.

"How are the children?" Koko asked.

"They are fine." Peter said.

"You must look after them," Koko said.

"We try Koko," Peter replied, biting another chunk from the apple. "But you know things are hard these days. Children don't listen anymore, and things are expensive."

Evelyn was tempted to say, "look who's talking," but she checked herself, and instead said, "That's why they need fathers to be there too."

Peter mumbled and got up to leave.

"Tell us if you hear anything," Evelyn said.

Neither of the women got up as he went out the back door.

"He's really strange," Evelyn said. "Sometimes, he irritates me for no good reason."

"He can be irritating. He keeps smiling, and doesn't know when to stop," Koko said. "He's family; what can we do? We just have to be patient. As the saying goes, every family has its own crazies."

"Oh, no. He knows what he's doing. He puts on this fake boyish charm so people will tolerate his rubbish," Evelyn said. "He doesn't buy food for his kids and he comes here and eats fruit when in his own house he doesn't buy it."

"Don't bother, let him eat all he wants," Koko said, "You know, food is nothing but dirt for the teeth."

"I'm always surprised that he's stuck with the Church youth theater club," Evelyn said. "Their Christmas nativity play last year was really wonderful."

"Reverend Nake is really gifted," Koko said. "I don't know how he persuaded Peter to work with those young people."

"I wouldn't be surprised if he's embezzling their meager funds." Evelyn said. "Raising money in their name."

"Ah…they all embezzle. As long as he does good work and leaves a few pennies for the club, "Koko said. "What can we say?"

Evelyn felt tempted to talk about how he mistreats his family but she stopped herself.

Koko left and Evelyn got back to her gardening. The sun was going down and there was still so much to do.

CHAPTER 4

Neo Receives Letter

Neo Maru cherished her new boarding school, Moroka High in Thaba Nchu, a whole day's driving from Pretoria. One of the good things about being in Moroka was that the drowning nightmares came less frequently. And when they did come, they were less virulent. She often outran whatever chased her, and in the water she was able to stay afloat or swim to safety.

Sometimes she missed the food at home, especially good cabbage, thinly sliced and sautéed with onions in butter and oil, and sprinkled with white pepper and salt.

Lunch was her favorite meal, because that's when mail was delivered at the dining hall. Not that she expected any mail on this particular day.

Her eyes struggled to adjust to the glare of the gleaming silver canisters that sat at the head of each long wooden table. The dim dining hall, with its beige walls, had high ceilings and windows far above their heads. After everybody entered and stood at their place at table, the Chief Prefect, on the stage announced, "Let's pray."

Heads bowed.

"For the food we are about to receive, we thank you, Lord. Amen," he said.

A long weary 'Amen' followed.

The long benches scraped over the cement floor as students took their seats. There was the sound of clanking metal spoons and plates as the Prefect dished out the porridge, beans and cabbage. The scent of burnt stiff cornmeal porridge and boiled cabbage filled the air. The place hummed like a swarm of locusts passing overhead.

Breakfast was only bread, tea, and soft porridge. Neo's stomach was usually shriveled by the time lunch came around. The lunch bell was always welcome. She ate fast, her mind completely absorbed in the task of filling her growling stomach.

When the Prefect who distributed the mail left two letters at her table, Neo hoped one of them would be hers. Maybe her pocket money was arriving a little early that month. It would be good because she was almost broke.

When she got the ivory envelope, she half expected to pass it on, when she realized it was hers. She could not open it immediately though, since it was against the rules to open letters in the dining hall.

She recognized the cursive writing with easy-flowing strokes, letters all the same size, leaning forward evenly. The tails at the end of each word were restrained, not wild. The total effect was clear and neat. One might even say beautiful, but in a quiet, rather than flashy way. It was from home, from Ntate, her father. She was surprised to get another letter from Ntate before she had replied to the previous one, but she was happy.

The address was written with a pen and ink, not a ball-point. She remembered how he used to say, "Ball-point pens encourage bad handwriting, that's why penmanship is a dying art." She remembered how earlier on Ntate, had worked hard at trying to improve her handwriting, and urged her to produce perfectly rounded O's and to cross T's at exactly the same point each time, not in the middle and not too high up. It did not work. Her handwriting continued to look like a fly dipped in ink had just walked haphazardly all over the page. In desperation she had asked her mother to teach her how to write beautifully.

"It just needs to be clear and legible," Mummy, had said, "not everybody can write as beautifully as your father. Just work on being legible, and don't worry about it."

"Don't be discouraged," Ntate had said, during one of these writing sessions, "you know what they say, practice makes perfect. Slow down, take your time."

As soon as she got outside the dining hall, she ripped the envelope and pulled out the letter. She walked slowly as she read.

"My Dear Daughter, I'm glad you've settled down and you like your new school.

Koko was here the other day and she sends her love. She said to remind you not to forget your night prayers. Yes, it's all right to write to me in English sometimes so you can practice. And yes, I'd be happy to read your Setswana stories anytime. It is important to learn to use your language well. It will make everything easier. Once you learn to manipulate your language well, it will be easier for you to manipulate English and other languages too. Also don't forget to study Afrikaans too. You don't want it to bring your final scores down."

Neo paused when she came to the line about Afrikaans. She hated Afrikaans. Afrikaners were bad. Everybody knew it. They were always rude. She continued to read the letter.

"Everybody is well here at home, except your brother Tiro was arrested at school with some of his friends. There is nothing to worry about; they'll probably be out soon. We'll know soon if or when the trial will be held. The whole thing has to do with some political events. We'll find out soon what it's all about."

Neo stopped. It was like a punch in the stomach. This news made her sick. She held her breath and clutched her throat to stop her food from coming up further. She took a deep breath, sighed and rubbed her burning eyes. People got arrested, but her brother? She read the line again just to make sure she'd really understood. Nobody in her family had ever been arrested. Tiro? No.

She continued reading.

"We went to see your grandmother at Fafung last weekend and she also sends her love. She thinks of you and wishes to hear about your new school when you get back.

Mummy says she'll send you a surprise package soon. Everybody misses you here at home.

Your Loving Father,

Ntate."

Neo continued to walk towards the dormitories. The main building was yellow brick and square-shaped. There was only one door to the complex and she passed the matron's flat on the left and the first dorm on the right, and entered a courtyard surrounded by other dormitories.

She walked past this main building and around to the freshman dormitory at the back, a nine year old temporary structure made out of corrugated iron-icy-cold in the winter, and as hot as Satan's fire in the summer. The roof was corrugated iron with no ceiling.

She went into the long tunnel-like dormitory and walked towards her bed at the furthest end. She sat on her bed, careful not to disturb the sharp edges, which reminded her of hospitals. The rows of beds looked like army barracks.

Neo carefully took out the letter, as though it were a bomb that would explode if not handled properly. She pressed it flat with her hand and started to read again.

Her friend Daisy came over. "Did you get a letter?"

Neo nodded without raising her gaze.

"From home?"

Another nod.

"Is it bad news?"

"My brother Tiro has been arrested," Neo whispered.

"Did he forget to carry his pass?" Daisy asked.

Neo shifted around on the edge of the bed. "Don't know. Maybe there was a strike like at your brother's school."

Daisy sat on the floor, faced Neo and leaned her back against the adjacent bed and said, "The police kept my brother for six days and then they sent him back to his school."

Neo looked at Daisy. "Maybe the same thing will happen to Tiro."

Daisy nodded her head vigorously. "Yes."

The bell rang, heavier than the milkman's bell at home, but lighter than the church bell. She took the letter and hurried to class for study period. She opened the geography textbook to the page on the "Forests of the World." On the opposite page, was a picture of big trees crowded together. Never having seen a forest before, Neo wondered if any people had been lost inside the forest or eaten by snakes.

She could see the dark belly of the forest where the rays of the sun never penetrated. She imagined a dark windowless cell where her brother sat against a wall, with his feet on the floor. His knees pressed tightly against his chest, and his arms were wrapped tightly around them. He buried his head inside his arms.

She placed the open letter inside on the picture of the dark forest, and read it again, being careful to make sure the letter did not hang out of the book. Reading non-school material during study time was a punishable offense—four marks, the equivalent of working on the dinner dish-washing crew two nights.

Maybe her brother, Kagiso, knew more about this arrest. She stared at the prefect, John, a senior student in the same class as Kagiso, also a prefect. John sat in front at the teacher's table. He leaned over to the left side and his elbow was propped straight against the wide dark wooden table and the side of his head rested in his hand.

Neo went up to him and asked for permission to go see her brother in his senior class.

"Do you have to go now?" John asked. "Are you all right?"

Neo coughed to give herself time to think up an excuse and then said, "Please, I'll never ask again."

"Is it something I can help you with?"

"Can't tell a boy."

"But, Kagiso is a boy too."

"But, he's my brother."

John smiled and said, "OK, go, hurry up, and don't linger outside."

Neo ran out. The main school building, brownish red, was shaped like a half-moon. She walked on the stoop from her classroom which anchored one end, past a string of classrooms, past the principal's office in the middle facing the main gate, and past the teachers staff rooms. The doors to the two staff rooms were beside each other, and Mr. van der Merwe, her Afrikaans teacher, leaned on the post separating the two doors on the white side. Her Setswana teacher, Mr. Senne, leaned against the same post on the black side.

She picked up her pace when she saw them to show she was purposeful. She darted across the coarse lawn and into the senior class building. She stood in front of the closed door of Kagiso's classroom for a moment to calm her racing heart.

She placed the back of her hand flat against the light grainy wooden door and tapped. She waited a moment. Her heart pumped furiously as though it were about to explode through her ribs. She took a deep breath and tapped hard with her knuckles.

When Kagiso came out she handed him the letter.

"It says Tiro has been arrested," she said.

"I know." He bit his lower lip and scanned the letter. "Oh yes, I received one too."

Neo's eyes narrowed. "Let me see your letter."

He looked away momentarily, his eyes shifting. He hesitated, and then said, "I left it at the dormitory."

"Will you show it to me tomorrow?"

He adjusted his collar and patted it all round to make sure it was flat. "It's just like yours, nothing different." He folded her letter carefully and gave it back.

"I thought maybe yours was longer with more details," she said. "How long is it, how many pages?"

He rubbed his temple as though he was massaging his brain, working hard to remember. "Short, just two or three pages, you know Ntate writes big sometimes and takes a lot of space."

"What did Ntate say?"

"Nothing much, just that Tiro has been arrested, like he said in your letter," he said. "The rest is just things here and there, nothing to do with Tiro."

"Things about home?"

"No, just about me," he said. "My plans for next year—college, work, you know." He scratched inside his left ear.

She still wanted to see the letter, but it was odd how he was uncomfortable answering easy questions. She wondered what he was hiding. "Why did they arrest Tiro? Did he do anything?"

"It's not clear yet," he said. "It's probably some small thing."

"Like forgetting a pass or something like that?"

"Something like that, but maybe not exactly the same thing," he said. "There's nothing to worry about. He'll be out soon."

"We'll see him when we go home for the June holidays." She tried to sound calm, pretending to have no doubts.

She clasped her hands and rested them on top of her head. Kagiso smiled and took both her hands. "Remember what they say about carrying your hands on your head?" In Setswana culture clasping hands above the head was a sign of deep loss and crying, usually at the death of parents or a provider. Doing it when there was no death could bring bad luck and result in the death of a parent.

Neo raised her voice. "I know!"

She looked away. Thank God she had Mummy and Ntate, she thought. A lightning stroke of fear flashed through her.

Kagiso put his index finger on his mouth. "Ssh, people are studying."

Neo stomped her foot. "If they are concentrating then they won't hear things that are none of their business," she said loudly.

"Neo, you know better than that, but it's all right."

She just stared at him.

Kagiso punched his right fist into his left hand in affected joviality.

"Go back to class," he said. "Time for homework."

She didn't move. She looked into his eyes, searched them carefully. Since the eyes were a window to the soul, she thought they might also be a window into the mind.

"I'll walk you to class. Remember the last assembly they warned about too much loitering during study period?" he said. "Let's walk fast to show we are busy."

They hurried to her class. He held the door handle and looked at her. She looked at him and thought he was going to say something.

"Don't worry, Neo," he whispered, "It's going to be all right. You've seen a lot of people go to jail and come back." He spoke very fast, like it was a heavy load and he wished to put it down quickly.

She sighed. "I guess so."

He opened the door and she went in. She grinned at John, the prefect, who looked beyond her, towards the door at Kagiso. John got out of his chair and went outside with Kagiso. They closed the door behind them.

The students started whispering.

John opened the door, stuck his head in and said, "Everybody be quiet and study." There was silence in the class, but not in Neo's head.

Through the streaked window she saw Kagiso and John talking and she wished she could hear them. They were serious at first with John nodding several times, and then they smiled, restrained smiles. As they parted, John patted Kagiso twice on the back. John came back in and Kagiso walked back towards his class. Neo watched him through the window until he was out of sight.

She stared at the forest picture in her book again and it drew her deep inside, into a dark cell. Tiro and his friends stood packed in tightly like the trees in the thick forest. They stretched their necks, trying to gasp for air.

Like their father, Tiro was three inches shorter than Kagiso. But Tiro looked stronger, with firm well-defined thighs and biceps. His cheekbones were higher than Kagiso's making his face appear harder. Tiro's jaw was firm as though his teeth were clenched tightly. He kept his hair short and tucked his shirt into his pants neatly, even when cleaning, cooking, or working in the yard. Tiro always walked upright and his hands swung in a controlled way, like a soldier.

The only time he seemed to let go completely was when he played soccer. He always played soccer, at home, at school, everywhere. He was his school's soccer champion. In his red and white uniform he was transformed. He dribbled so fast your eyes worked hard to keep up with the ball. He dodged between other players like it was the easiest thing to do. When he flew into the sky to head a ball, he soared like an eagle. During those magic moments the spectators roared "Pro!" his soccer name. He had already been picked to play for Melodi Swallows, the number one team in the soccer league that year.

Neo placed the letter inside the book and read it again.

"Koko was here the other day and she sends her love. She said to remind you not to forget your night prayers."

Neo missed Koko. She was the one person who always understood her fully and who could always smooth the wrinkles of fear inside her until there was calm. One of the last conversations they had shortly before Neo left for boarding school had been about Kilnerton, both the High School and the village.

"It is a pity you won't be going to Kilnerton like everybody," Koko said, narrowing her eyes. "You were born a little late. Both your parents went there, and now it's closed."

"It's all right, Koko," Neo said. "I get to go far in Moroka. It will be fun."

"And the village," Koko said, "they took our houses and fields and everything for nothing, the Boers."

"One day the revolution will come," Neo said, echoing the talk of the older boys on the street. "And, we'll send them all back to their Europe."

Koko smiled the indulgent smile one gives young people one loves dearly when they talk simply about complicated matters.

Koko became serious. "The church at Kilnerton was the best church," Koko said. "You were all baptized there. You were baptized by Reverend Goba. He was the best. When he preached, the walls shook." When she said this she held up both her fists and moved them as though she was shaking something.

Neo heard the story before but she didn't mind because each time a new detail would emerge. Koko was the person who had the patience to talk about the period of her life Neo didn't remember.

"And then, there was the Rev. Wilson, who was head of the whole Methodist Church circuit around Pretoria all the way to Witbank. He was the only white minister who could preach in Xhosa. Remarkable man, that Wilson. If you closed your eyes you'd think that it was a black man preaching...different kind of white man he was...had a heart, not like the others...true man of God." Koko shook her head. "There aren't ministers like that anymore," she said. "The ones with God's fire burning inside them."

Neo reflected on the fact that all Koko's children and her son-in-law Edward, had gone to Kilnerton High School and

Kilnerton Teacher-Training College never moving far from Kilnerton Village.

"Koko, why didn't everyone just refuse to move from Kilnerton?" Neo said. "You should have refused to move, Koko."

"They would have bulldozed our houses and arrested us and maybe even banned us," Koko said. "They even moved our graves."

Koko's eyes narrowed and assumed a far-away look. She looked down. "They moved your grandfather's grave," she said, and shook her head. "White people are strange, they have no respect for sacred things, not even for the dead."

"But, Koko, aren't the Boers Christian?" Neo asked. "Aren't they afraid God will punish them for moving graves?"

Koko paused for a while, pondering the question, trying to find a way to explain the inexplicable.

The bell rang ending study period. Neo jumped, snapping out of her reverie. Neo walked to the dormitory alone.

That night, Neo prayed the Lord's prayer and added a prayer for Tiro. In a dream, Neo was chased by a windowless dark gray truck. Towards the back it looked like an oil tanker and in front it had a big nose like an army tank. She ran on the narrow road until she came to the edge of the river. The road jutted into the river and formed a V shape at the end. At the sharp point which was the edge of the river, the road was just wide enough for her two feet and the water almost touched her. A short distance away in the river, the white woman, Mamogashwa waved to her.

The truck groaned like the army tanks that paraded in the townships when there were strikes, and in the river dark waves roared and thrashed and splashed her with jets of cold water. Just as the tank was about to hit her, Neo jumped into the water and the tank stopped abruptly. She paddled near the riverbank to avoid Mamogashwa, the snake. She also watched the armored tank, hoping that it didn't come in after her. Then, she would have to swim along the edge and into deeper water.

She flailed about and kicked hard with her legs, struggling to keep her head above the water. Each time she grabbed a drifting tree limb to hold on to, it would break away.

Finally, the truck retreated unable to follow her into the water. She hoisted herself onto land and woke up panting and damp with sweat. She planted her feet on the cold cement floor. Good thing she slept with her legs stretched out.

One day she had told Koko that during nightmares she couldn't run.

"My feet get entangled around each other," Neo said. "And they get heavy and I can't outrun whatever is chasing me."

"Good you told me," Koko said. "You see, if you sleep with your legs straight and your body relaxed not curled over like a tight bundle, you will be able to run in your dreams. That way nothing bad can catch you."

The problem for Neo was to try and remember this advice when she went to bed.

She was used to Mamogashwa dreams where she knew to run when she saw the evil snake woman. This dream, being chased by police trucks and army tanks, was new. She'd have to write to Koko to get tips about dealing with police trucks in dreams.

CHAPTER 5

Travel Plans

Waiting was hard. Evelyn hoped her son Tiro's detention would end soon so the family could see him. She worried about Edward. He always took things so hard, especially if it had to do with the children. Being the quiet, scholarly type, he brooded a lot and held things in.

Evelyn had lots of friends and that kept her busy and gave her support. But she was afraid for Edward. She believed the old saying that quiet people who held things inside, could drop dead suddenly.

Worse, Edward taught at a university with only three other black people on staff, so he had little support. Not that he talked about it much, but Evelyn could imagine how hostile his white colleagues must have been. Even though more qualified, Edward had not been promoted because his promotion would have meant his being above some white colleagues. Evelyn was glad that his one-week research trip to Botswana was coming up. It would give him a break, take him away from this whole mess, get him out of the pressure cooker.

Evelyn and Edward sat at the kitchen table. Evelyn poured tea into cups.

"Are you all ready for your trip?" she asked.

Edward rubbed the bald spot on his head. "Actually, I've been thinking, that I should postpone it."

"Why?" She asked though she already knew his answer.

"I don't see how I could go when things are so uncertain."

Evelyn handed him his cup of tea and pushed the milk jug and the sugar basin closer to him.

"You go ahead. It won't be hard to call you back if anything changes."

Edward shifted in his chair.

"There's nothing to do right now anyway," Evelyn continued. The lawyer said we can't do anything, so there's really no point in staying here."

Evelyn really wanted him to go. She was trying to ease him out of the pressure-cooker.

"You already went to all the trouble to arrange this." Evelyn said.

"Leave you alone?" Edward said, "No."

"I'm all right. Go ahead."

The Botswana trip was just three days away; the preparations would keep him busy.

The next afternoon when Evelyn returned from work, she saw a white car parked in front of her gate. She opened the gate and three white men and a black man got out of the car and walked towards her.

"Evelyn Maru?" A white man said.

"Yes," Evelyn said. "Can I help you?"

"Can we talk inside?" The tall white man in a safari suit spoke this time. "We are security police."

Her heart sank, but she quickly recovered. Maybe they'd tell her about Tiro's case or maybe they'd say when he'd be released.

Inside the living room, she offered them seats, but they declined.

"Is this about my son Tiro?"

"Yes, we'd like to search the house," the tall man in the safari suit said.

Evelyn looked up and down at the black officer who stood with his chest thrust forward. His eyes were red. She despised his type more than any of the others, but she bit her tongue. They had her son and this fool might take out his anger on Tiro.

The policemen went into the front bedroom and started rummaging through drawers. They searched the wardrobe. The black man searched the bottom drawer and pulled out all the documents and threw them on the bed.

Evelyn stood at the door. Eagerly they all crowded around the documents. They flipped through the birth certificate, baptismal certificate and other papers. One white officer read the passports. He tossed one passport on the bed and pocketed the other. Then, they looked under the mattress. Next they moved to the boys room and didn't come out with anything. Finally, they went into Neo's room but they didn't spend much time there.

They nodded and walked towards the door without a word.

"All you had to do was ask." Evelyn said. "I would've pulled out the passports and saved you all this work."

"It's our job to look," the youngest white man said. "We are taking his passport."

"When can my husband get it back?" Evelyn said.

"We don't know," the one in the safari suit said." We're taking it to the head office."

The police marched back to their car and drove off without looking back.

Evelyn waited until she could no longer see the car then she sat down in the kitchen and kicked off her shoes. A current swirled in her head. She thought of Edward—what was this going to do to him? After a minute, she walked to her bedroom and stood at the door, surveying the mess.

"The dogs," she said angrily. She began to put away the documents and garments strewn through the room. She worked fast; she didn't want Edward to find the house torn apart. He'd be devastated. How was she going to break the news about the passport to him? Evelyn sat on the bed and sighed deeply. After a while she went to the kitchen and started cooking.

When Edward arrived from work Evelyn followed him to the bedroom.

"The Security Police were here," she said.

Edward took a deep breath. "What did they want?"

"The brutes," she said. "They took your passport."

"Can't go to Botswana now anyway," he said. "Not with things so uncertain."

She was surprised Edward took this news calmly. But, she knew it was because he was torn about going to Botswana. With the passport gone the decision was out of his hands. She knew that the house search did bother him. They were being treated like criminals. But Evelyn was relieved he took it so well.

After dinner they sat around the kitchen table for a while and then retired to bed early.

CHAPTER 6

George In Moroka

Neo and Daisy liked to take walks in the late afternoon before dinner. One afternoon around five they walked from the dormitory on the footpath towards the soccer field. When they came to within ten yards of the field, they turned around. Beyond that point was out of bounds for girls. They saw Reverend Williams and his wife.

"Look, they walk so fast. They act like they're being chased by monsters," Neo said.

Daisy nodded. "Strange people."

Reverend Williams walked upright with a long stride that appeared out of step with his short height, and swung his wooden cane in the precise manner of a drum major. His short legs seemed to have a motor separate from the rest of his body. He came from England and was head of the whole

Methodist Mission in Thaba N'chu, the boarding school and the hospital nearby.

Mrs. Williams was slightly taller, and wore a light blue shirt dress. She walked fast, but with shorter steps. Her clipped full brown hair was streaked with gray, around a face round and soft; her brown eyes were small and sharp. Her tight smile made her thin lips appear thinner. Her yorkshire terrier on a leash walked in tiny steps like a wind-up toy. It shook its head, tossing the hair out of its big eyes.

The Reverend and his wife both smiled and said in unison, "Good evening."

"Good evening, Governor, Ma'am," the girls said.

The dog barked and wagged its tail.

After they passed, Neo mocked them by speaking through her teeth with her mouth barely open. "Good evening."

Daisy thrust her chest forward and straightened her neck, in exaggerated imitation of Mrs. Williams' upright posture.

They laughed.

"And when they eat," Neo said, then simulated chewing, placing the tip of her finger in her mouth and pressed it slightly between her lips. "They eat like this."

Daisy laughed.

"The English don't eat much. Before they cook, they count food like carrots and string beans," Neo said. "If there's four people, they cook four potatoes, and if a visitor comes in while they're eating, they don't share the food. They give them tea and little biscuits you bite and chew with the front teeth, like a bird."

Daisy repeated her English eating act and laughed.

"They are nice, but stingy," Daisy said.

"The Boers are nasty, but they don't count food," Neo said.

"What does Governor do everyday?" Daisy asked.

Neo could only think of one thing. "Preach during Sunday evening service."

"Not every Sunday," Daisy said. "And why do they walk with the dog everyday? Why don't they give it to the boys to walk and play with?"

Neo remembered other talks about dogs with her friends-friends whose mothers worked as maids for white people in town. "They like to play with dogs," Neo said. "They take them to beauty shops where they wash them with sweet smelling soaps, comb their hair and the gardeners wash them sometimes"

"The dogs also lie with the people on their beds," Daisy added.

"My brother Pitso says you have to be careful with the English," Neo said. "They speak softly and they are good at smiling. They pat you on the back, and then put a dagger into you. He said Afrikaners don't pretend."

Daisy pounded Neo's back hard with her fist to show how the English dagger pierces.

"The Boers like to beat people and are never polite," Neo said, "They just snarl all the time so you know to run before they kill you."

Neo reflected for a moment and then continued. "The boers enjoy hurting people. That's why they like to be police-men." She thought of Tiro in police custody and felt sad.

The bell rang and it was time to go to dinner, and after-wards came evening study period.

One of the strictest rules at Moroka was the compulsory language rule. Mondays, Wednesdays and Fridays, the stu-dents spoke only English; Tuesdays and Thursdays only Afrikaans; Saturdays and Sundays they were free to speak any language, which meant Setswana since the school admitted only Setswana-speaking students.

Neo and Daisy were not surprised when Tuesday before Easter weekend, during a short break at ten-thirty in the morning, Joe, who had a scar over his left eye, joined them. He whispered in broken Afrikaans, "Mense is gevang," meaning "people have been arrested."

They huddled closer together, their heads in a bundle in the middle of a circle.

"*Wat*?" Daisy asked in Afrikaans.

"*In my dormitorie, hulle het Pitso gevang*" Peter went on. "They've arrested people in my dormitory."

"Wie is gevang? vir wat?" Neo said wanting to know who was arrested.

The bell rang before they could get the full story out of Joe. Conversation on Afrikaans days was slow and tortuous. Neo looked around and even though she didn't see a prefect, she was afraid to take a chance and risk being caught speaking Setswana on an Afrikaans day. It would have increased her punishment marks. She leaned into Peter's ear and spoke in Setswana, "Tell me quickly, who got arrested?"

Everybody huddled together tightly as Peter whispered in Setswana. "The police picked up several boys from the dorms before dawn."

"Why?" Neo asked.

"Don't know. Something to do with plotting a strike or starting trouble, maybe."

"A strike!" Daisy screamed.

"Shhh, don't get me into trouble, I don't know anything. I just hear things in the wind," Peter said.

They went into class and Mr. Seleka was late, so they had time to continue talking, adding new horrors, casting a dark mood.

Mr. Seleka finally strode in, and they stopped talking. He rummaged through his papers for a while, then, leaned against the desk and rested one hand on it.

"Pass your homework in, please," he said in a deep, tired voice.

He collected their books and tossed them on the table without counting them, which was unusual.

"Anybody not done their homework?" Mr. Seleka asked.

Two hands went up. To everyone's surprise, he didn't reprimand them or tell them to see him after class. Instead, he said, "OK, fine, just bring them next class."

He arranged his papers meticulously on the table, as though it was the most important thing in the world that the edges lined up perfectly. He took off his glasses, and rubbed the sides of his nose, and then took out a white handkerchief and wiped the glasses. His movements reminded Neo of her father.

The air in the class was thick. Neo quietly pushed the window next to her open. A thin, sharp breeze swept over her.

Mr. Seleka started to talk about the chapter in a novel he had assigned.

"Before we discuss this chapter, can someone summarize it briefly for us?"

There were no volunteers.

Neo looked down hoping it made her invisible.

"Neo," he called.

She cleared her throat and started to get up.

"It's all right, you don't have to stand," he said.

She sat down. "This chapter is about a young woman, Dineo, from Zeerust, who leaves her village for the first time to look for work in Johannesburg. She has heard about the bright lights of the city from her older cousin who has worked in Johannesburg for four years. She is-"

The principal suddenly stood at the door and Neo stopped talking. Mr. Seleka joined him and the principal whispered something. Two white men in suits and a black man in a black jacket and brown pants stepped into the room. The principal pointed towards the back and in Afrikaans said, "George, *kom.*"

George left his seat and strutted towards the front. Before he went out the door, he glanced back. His eyes had a fiery intensity like he desperately wanted to say something deep, something that couldn't be put into words.

Neo's eyes burned. She thought of Tiro. That must be how he was arrested.

Mr. Seleka slumped to the table and sat on his chair. He rubbed his eyes with both hands and looked sleepily at Neo.

Someone sneezed. Others cleared their throats, a few had sniffles.

"Neo," he said in a tired voice. "Continue. Start from the beginning."

She cleared her throat. "The story is about a young woman who prepares to go to the city."

Her voice quivered. Her throat felt as though it had a ball of clay stuck in it. When she heard sobbing, she stopped, and looked around. Daisy was one of the girls crying. Neo rested her elbow on the desk, bent her head and covered her eyes with her hands.

"It's all right, Neo," Mr. Seleka said. "Everybody read quietly. We'll continue tomorrow."

Neo's tears rained into her hands. The tears gushed like someone opened a powerful faucet. She forgot where she was, as if she were caught in the rain in the open veld and she was alone. There was no shelter in sight. Around her most girls cried, and many boys fought tears in their eyes.

Nine boys were arrested that dark day.

A few days later, George limped back into class and took his seat silently. The students looked at him with awe as if he had just risen from the dead. During break, Neo and Daisy joined George, Joe, and Eric—all teammates on the junior soccer team.

"How come you're limping?" Daisy asked. "Did you fall?"

"I fell when they beat me up, shoving me from one policeman to the other," George said.

"Why?" Neo asked.

"Because they said I wasn't telling the truth," George said.

"What truth?" Daisy said.

"They asked about ring leaders who were plotting something," George said. "And, they wanted to know who they were."

"What did you say?" Neo asked.

George shrugged his shoulders. "Nothing. I didn't know anything."

"So?" Daisy said.

"They beat me up and called me a cheeky *Kaffir*. They kept asking me the same questions," George said. "Man, I thought I was gone six feet under. They said we Transvaal boys were causing trouble and hatching all kinds of plots."

"They're always accusing us of influencing everybody," Peter said. "Just because we come from the Transvaal, we are trouble to them."

"Where did they beat you?" Neo asked.

"Neo," Joe said in his deep voice and shook his head to stop her.

Neo ignored him. "They kicked you?" Neo asked.

"Everywhere," George answered wearily. "And, when you fall, they kick you more."

"The dogs," Joe said. "One day, they'll swim to their Europe."

George raised his shirt to show them the long purple marks on his back.

Neo held her head between her hands, and her eyes began to tear. "Uh!"

Daisy covered her mouth with one hand.

"I have to go to the toilet before the bell rings," George said.

He limped away. Neo was glad these boys had been released. This meant her brother Tiro had probably been released too; the next letter from Ntate would surely confirm it.

CHAPTER 7

Home Go

From early May, each night Neo scratched out the day on her calendar. 'Home go' finally arrived in June. She left her brother Kagiso who still had one more day of exams.

Passengers headed to the Transvaal, her province, boarded the train to Bloemfontein that left Thaba 'Nchu station at six in the morning. The light started to peek from behind the mountain by the time the train pulled out of the station. It was a special student-only local commuter train, without sleeping compartments. Students sat on wooden benches on both sides of the center aisle.

As the steam train chugged away, the students crowded at the windows and waved at the group of senior boys who helped with the departure. The boys waved back, some with handkerchiefs. Neo's brother waved until the train was out of sight. Even after the boys were no longer in view, Neo and her friends kept waving at the dark mountains.

In the dim light of dawn, the mountain seemed to grow from the ground; and as the morning brightened, the mountain seemed to anchor and assert a stronger self. The train rolled along in the shadow of the mountain for close to an hour.

Neo sat by the window, facing forward and Daisy sat directly facing her. The train trembled like the tracks had bumps on them. The car shook in all directions. The wheels clickety-clacked and rattled like pieces of metal being shaken in a tin can. The weak yellow sun filtered through the streaked window. The naked willows and poplars rushed past. The dew on the rusty grass glistened in the sunlight. Neo fixed her eyes on the mountain, and after a while, the mountain moved, but not the train.

About two hours later, at eight the train pulled into Bloemfontein Station where they waited forty-five minutes before boarding the train to Germiston.

This new train was a diesel with a huge engine, like the head of a hippopotamus. The Germiston train was a long-distance train with compartments, singles for three people and doubles for six people. Neo shared a compartment with Daisy. It was day, so they didn't open the beds.

At eight-fifteen, the train pulled out of Bloemfontein Station. The great engine, like a gathering thunderstorm, rumbled deeply and slowly. As it accelerated it settled down and roared with a steady rhythm.

They cut through the industrial area of Bloemfontein where they saw smoke stacks and the backs of old buildings with dusty signs. At crossings, the locomotive's siren pierced the air like a razor.

Then, they heard "kaartjies, kaartjies". A white guard in black and white uniform with shiny silver buttons, stepped into their compartment and clipped their tickets.

After they left Bloemfontein, the train rolled through endless stretches of grassland and maize fields. Large brick farm houses were scattered about. Small towns, with one-room stations, swept by. Where the gold of the dead grass and corn stalks met the clear blue sky was a dense reddish glow as if all the colors of the rainbow danced there.

Once they left the mountains of Thaba 'Nchu, the Orange Free State province was flat grassland, like one huge maize field. In the summer it was a continent of green, and now in the winter month of June, a blanket of gray.

The weather was cold. The fields looked desolate like nothing would ever grow again. Neo stared at the drooping burnt cornstalks that seemed to weep in the merciless winter winds.

The train finally stopped at a small one room station, named Parys, its station sign in fading green letters. Black men, watched by a white man in a khaki hat, loaded polished stainless steel milk cans onto the train.

When Neo first went to boarding school in January of nineteen-sixty-three, a month before her thirteenth birthday, she had pictured this day of returning as one of joy. She had dreamt of her first trip home as a triumphant event after succeeding in school and thriving on her own for the first time. Instead, she was on the train, anxious about what home was going to be like with her brother Tiro missing. She couldn't be happy when Tiro wouldn't be home. That would've been a betrayal. Home was unraveling, maybe falling apart, and it seemed like her having left home might have caused it. All the time she had been home nothing of consequence had ever gone wrong and her brothers were always safe.

The train rocked along through the fields and Neo drifted in and out of sleep.

Daisy slapped Neo's knee. "We're getting close to the Vaal River, we're nearly home."

A student in the corridor shouted, "Vaal River, Vaal River!" They were leaving behind the Orange Free State, home of the 'real' Afrikaner, who, according to reputation, sported a tanned face, wore a short safari suit and stood ready to crack the sjambok on any black person at the slightest chance. It seemed like a land where every white man acted like a policeman.

Neo and Daisy stood by a window in the corridor, crowded by fellow students.

The train crawled as it neared the long bridge and wallowed across like an overburdened ox. Soft crystalline light bounced off the surface of the gray-black water, a soft shimmer as the sun set and lost its fire. In the middle of the bridge, the train slowed down even more, and trembled as though it was struggling to stay on the tracks.

Neo trembled.

What if they got stuck in the middle of the bridge, and the bridge gave way, and the train spilled into the river? She spotted something dark and slimy in the water. She blinked hard, but it was gone. Maybe the Vaal River had its own big snake, like Mamogashwa in Moretele River in Melodi, her home township.

At last, the train crossed the bridge and picked up speed for a short while, before slowing down for Vereeniging Station, the first town in the Transvaal. An hour later, the train pulled into the last stop, Germiston Station, where they changed for Pretoria.

Germiston Station was dim inside. It was the end of the day and the black side of the station pulsed with people streaming in all directions. Women carried children on their backs. Miners from Lesotho lugged tin trunks. Draped over their shoulders, were blankets with bold strokes of orange, light brown, gold, and blue. Fashionably dressed young women in high heels and tight skirts swayed their hips; young men in suits and ties folded *The World* or *Daily Mail* under their arms. Young boys, bent under big boxes of apples shouted, "*Diapola, diapola,* two for five cents." A railway policeman in brown uniform marched up and down the platform.

"The World, The World," a young black man shouted, hawking the country's only national paper for blacks, owned by a white company.

Another shouted, *"The Mail!, The Mail!"* The Rand Daily Mail, was an English daily paper.

Neo and Daisy hugged and kissed good-bye. Daisy was going to take a train to Springs, her home town. Neo wished Daisy was coming with her.

"Don't forget to write," Daisy said, with tears in her eyes.

Neo struggled to hold back her tears, but one huge drop rolled down her cheek. It almost felt like the end of the world and not just a good-bye.

"I'm going to write to you tomorrow," Neo said.

"Me too," Daisy said.

Neo gathered her bags and walked down the stairs into the dim tunnel with its musty acidic smell. She waded over dirty brown paper packets, crumpled newspapers, cigarette butts and other trash to platform fourteen to catch the train home.

Through speakers, a deep heavy voice broadcast in English, Afrikaans, Sotho, and Zulu. "Train on platform fourteen, the train to Pretoria, express first stop Kempton Park, Thembisa and Pretoria."

After the diesel train, the fast electric commuter train seemed to glide on the tracks. It whipped through smoke stacks, mounds of gold dust, drab concrete factories, and white towns. For Neo everything appeared the same, as dull grayish images swept by the train window. Her head bobbed back and forth. After forty five minutes the train pulled into Pretoria station-at last!

Neo's father was there to meet her.

"*Ngwanake*," he called to her in Setswana. They kissed and hugged.

Calling her "my child" soothed her, but Neo also remembered he often used "my child" when he was about to tell her something that would not please her. It was like he was trying to soothe her before giving her bitter medicine.

"Ntate," Neo said.

She thought Ntate looked darker and thinner than when she last saw him. His face looked long and his cheekbones seemed more exposed. His eyes seemed more deeply set. His brow was shiny even though it was cool. There were furrows on his forehead. But, his smile comforted her.

"How are you?" Edward asked.

"Fine. Good," she said.

"I'm parked just outside. Let's go my child."

They got into the car, a cream blue medium-size Vauxhall Velox. He started to back out of the parking spot, but braked abruptly as a car appeared suddenly and passed at high speed. Neo held on to the dashboard.

"These young people are crazy behind the wheel," Edward said. "How can anyone drive like this in a parking lot?"

"He's a white pig!" Neo shouted.

"Neo!" Edward said. "What kind of language-"

Neo thought a lecture was going to follow. She was relieved when her father did not continue.

He touched her arm, trying to calm her.

"Look at all the people," Neo said as though she was in the city for the first time.

"Peak hour, everybody is going home," he said.

"You know, there's no real town in Thaba 'Nchu," she said. "There's just one corner with a few stores clustered around it, nothing much. People go to Bloemfontein to do major shopping."

"It's a lovely peaceful place," Edward said.

They stopped at a red light on van der Walt street. The light turned green and they started to drive forward. A young black man dashed in front of the car. Edward braked, and Neo grabbed the dashboard. Cars blasted their horns.

"That poor man is probably rushing for the bus or the train," Edward said. "Some people live so far."

They were quiet for a few minutes before Edward asked, "How was your trip?" Ntate asked.

"Good." She couldn't postpone talking about her brother. "How is Tiro?"

"He's fine. We saw him yesterday, he is healthy," Edward said in a calm voice. "How were the exams?"

"Good," Neo said quickly. "When is he coming home?"

Edward cleared his throat, squared his shoulders and sat tall, as though he was trying to see the road better. He shifted gears. "There is going to be a trial."

Neo sat up straight. "A trial? What did he do?"

Edward accelerated. "It's political. We'll talk about all this when we get home." He braked, slowing the car down. "Over the speed limit, they are ticketing mercilessly these days. So, tell me about your exams, were they hard?"

The world's sounds were muffled in Neo's ears, as though her father's voice was being thrown from afar. She saw her brother in handcuffs. She blinked and squeezed her eyes hard

Her father's strong voice startled her. "Neo, how were the exams, were they hard?"

"No, they were all right," Neo said. "The boys they arrested at our school were all released. How come Tiro is not released?"

"Well, it is different. His situation is a little more complicated. Politics."

"Is Pitso home?"

"Yes, and he's fine. You'll see him. Everybody is fine."

Neo felt like screaming, "Nobody's fine!" But she controlled herself.

Pretoria was ugly. The jacaranda trees, when she left in January were in full bloom with light blue-purple flowers. Their delicate flowers had covered the streets and infused the air with a sweet soothing perfume. Now, they were bare, their leaves burned by the cold wind.

A few miles past the Union Buildings, they passed *The Doll House*, a drive-through restaurant where whites were served in their cars. For another mile or so, there were no buildings on either side of the road until Silverton, a suburb of Pretoria.

Neo pointed to the left as they passed the gate that used to be the entrance to Kilnerton High School and Teacher Training College.

"There's Kilnerton," she said, as though her father had forgotten where he went to school and used to teach long ago. This was the same school her brother Tiro had gone to. But, it was forced by the government to close because the area had been declared 'white'. The village around it, where all the Maru children were born, was given to white people.

"What is going to become of Kilnerton?" Neo asked.

"We don't know. Some say its going to be razed and a private white school built on it. Some say they are going to build houses for white people."

"There's where our house used to be," Neo said, pointing to big new houses.

Neo didn't say it, but she wished Mamogashwa, the woman-snake, would pass over the houses during a storm and flatten them. But then she remembered Mamogashwa was white, and would therefore not attack white people.

They continued in silence and passed Checkers Supermarket, the Silverton Bakery, Edwork Shoe Store and a Greek-owned cafe, called Spartans.

They drove over a small bridge across a shallow river and turned left towards Melodi. On the right was the new white suburb of Littleton. Black people called it 'Congo'. It was established by government subsidies to house white people fleeing African countries after their independence.

The houses were modest by white standards—three bedroom brick houses, with flat roofs and small yards. The streets were tarred and narrow.

"Congo has grown and already people are living there," Neo said.

"More and more are arriving every day, the place is growing fast."

"You know," Neo said. "These are the worst white people, worse than the white people who have been here long."

"How so?" her father asked, with a quick glance.

"I mean white people not born in South Africa are real bad," she said, "The ones who are from Europe were nothing in their countries and now here they have Africans to lord it over. The ones from places like Kenya and Nigeria are used to oppressing Africans. Now, they can't do it anymore 'cause of independence, so they run here." Neo said this speech so fast, she was out of breath by the end.

Edward sighed.

"Well," he began in his usual slow and deliberate way, as though he had all the time in the world. "It's not so simple. Even among white people, there are some decent people."

She frowned. "White people are all devils, we should throw them into the ocean and have them swim to their Europe."

"That wouldn't be kind," Edward said. "Not a Christian thing to do."

"They are not Christian," she said. "They are just devils. Their God is white like them, and evil too."

He braked, changed gears, and slowed as they approached the bridge over the train tracks. Then, they entered, Melodi.

A wave of Black people poured out of Denneboom Station onto the street, dodging lorries, cars, bicycles, and buses at the corner.

Neo had not seen such crowds in a while. "So many people."

A police van stood at the entrance to the station, and police checked men's passes. Three green Putco buses were swallowing long lines of people headed to other areas of the township. A line of taxis waited to ferry people who could afford to pay a little more and get home faster.

A taxi cut in front of them.

"Look how many people there are in that taxi," Neo said. "Must be eight people."

"You have to get out of the way of taxis this time of day," Ntate said. "This is when they make their money."

A traffic officer pulled the taxi over.

"Probably going to cite him for overloading," Edward said. "Poor man."

"I hate it when I'm in the taxi and they pack us like that," Neo said. "He should give the Traffic officer a little something, then he won't get a ticket."

Edward smiled. "Now, Neo how do you know that?"

Neo laughed. "Everybody knows that."

The air was thick with the acid smoke from coal stoves which irritated Neo's nose.

At the next intersection they turned right. They passed the men's hostel, a compound of brick buildings, square like a fort. Male migrant laborers lived there as "temporary sojourners", until they were too old to work. Because of the Influx Control Laws they couldn't rent a house and bring their families to live with them; the government considered their kin 'superfluous appendages." The Marus were one of the lucky families who were from this area and had the right to live in Melodi.

Down the street was the cemetery, the Western border of Melodi which separated it from the colored township of Derdepoort.

They left the tarred road and turned right onto a dusty unpaved street. Edward swerved to avoid a pothole. They weren't so bad in the winter, but the rains that year fell through autumn and the roads hadn't been fixed. In the summer, rain turned the streets into tributaries, flowing towards the Moretele River that divided the township into east and west.

Edward and Neo passed row upon row of four-room brick houses with corrugated iron roofs. They were packed tightly on top of each other like matchboxes, the monotony occasionally broken by a larger house on a big corner lot. Many yards had peach trees, a few had vines.

Through the dark smoke over the township, the setting sun hung, a deep, menacing red-brownish shade around it.

The Maru house, on the corner lot, jutted into an inter-section. If a driver came down the street at a high speed, and missed the curve, they might fly straight into the house. To prevent such an accident, Evelyn had planted a big cement block at the corner near the gate. That block damaged a lot of cars and saved the Maru house many times.

Like all streets in Melodi and other townships, their street had no name. Houses were identified by sections and numbers. Melodi was divided into seven sections; the Marus lived in Section Q. Their House number was 1206.

When the car stopped in front of the garage, Neo leapt and ran into the kitchen. She bathed in the warm air that held a rich curry aroma, spiced with cinnamon. This was home. Evelyn kissed her and gave her a big hug and laughed her usual hearty laugh.

"You've grown," Evelyn said, stroking the right side of Neo's face. "And you look healthy and radiant. Thaba 'Nchu loves you."

Neo scrutinized her mother's eyes. "Ntate says Tiro's not home yet."

"No. Not yet, but soon we hope."

"Where's Pitso?" Neo asked.

"Just went out for a while."

"Maybe Pitso can walk me to Koko's house."

Evelyn brushed Neo's shoulders lightly. "Too late, besides, we'd like to see you too. You can go first thing in the morning. She sent some scones this afternoon to welcome you home."

Neo missed Koko; she would reassure her about everything that was going on.

"More things to bring in?" Neo asked.

Edward motioned with his hand. "No no, sit down. There's just my book bag," he said. "I'll get it."

"Want some hot Milo?" Evelyn asked, "We'll have dinner as soon as Pitso comes in."

Edward went to his room.

Neo stood at the stove and took the lid off each pot and sniffed. "Mm…curried chicken, rice, peas, squash. Mummy, do you know I haven't had real rice since I left in January? No chicken either. We only had mielie-rice on Sundays, with beef stew."

"Mielie rice is nice, it's almost just like rice," Evelyn said.

"I don't like it much, but it's better than stiff maize porridge everyday," Neo said. "Mummy, I want to eat only rice, dumplings, chicken and such things. Only nice things. No more porridge for me."

"The food at your school is not too bad," Evelyn said. "Porridge is filling. And remember, a lot of children are starving."

"In prison also," Neo said.

Evelyn cleared her throat.

Edward came through the dining room door.

"You people think the food is bad?" He shook his head slowly and smiled. "Even in teacher training college, we didn't have any meat, except for maybe twice or thrice a month. You people have beef stew!"

"Only once a week in teacher training?" Neo said. "Better to go to the university."

"But Neo, you had other good things, like beans on the other days," Evelyn said. "Anyway, too much meat causes ringworm."

"That true?" Neo asked.

"That's what Koko says," Evelyn said.

The kitchen door opened and Pitso came in. Neo jumped from her chair and hugged him. His round eyes were red, making him look haggard. He had a thinner face than the other Maru children. He looked like Evelyn's father in the pictures. He was also a darker shade.

Tiro's absence seemed to intensify everybody's presence for Neo.

"Your friends have been waiting for you. Noli, Paula, all of them," Pitso said. He rubbed his stomach. "Hey, I'm starving."

Over dinner Neo brought up the subject of the trial. "Can I go to court tomorrow?"

Her mother quickly took a big bite of chicken, probably so she wouldn't have to answer, Neo thought.

Edward wiped his mouth with the yellow cloth napkin and spread it carefully on his lap. He cleared his throat. "We haven't discussed it. Your mother and I will talk about it after dinner and see." Edward looked sadly at Neo.

"I want to see him," Neo said. "At least in court we can see him even if it is at a distance."

"You can't get near them in court," Edward said. "After the proceedings, they whisk them off through the back immediately. Then, into vans and they drive away. Can't get close to them."

"At least we'll see him," Neo said. "I haven't seen him since January."

"Your mother and I need to talk about this," Edward said. "We aren't sure of things. There might be demonstrations, police dogs, and all that."

"I have to go, Ntate," Neo pleaded.

"I understand," Edward said. "I just worry about your safety.

"Maybe you should skip the first day of the trial," Evelyn added. "We'll see how things look, then maybe you can go."

Neo covered her face with her hands and started to cry.

"Neo," Edward said. "We also want you to go, and I'm sure your brother would like to see you there. We are just worried about your safety."

"I want to go," she whispered. "Please...please..."

Silence.

"All right," Evelyn said glancing at Edward first. "You'll go tomorrow. But I want you to promise that if there is any trouble, you won't go again."

"I promise," Neo said, breathless.

They ate the rest of the meal in silence.

After dinner they cleaned up the kitchen and sat around the stove.

For Neo, the house had an eerie feel to it—the way the air feels thick before a thunderstorm. Everybody seemed like part of an apparition. It was as though all of them, including herself, were wind-up dolls, part of a theater set, nothing real. She looked at the fire in the stove through the opening in front and it looked as though it wasn't just coals burning, but some other things as well; she didn't know what. The fire reminded her of pictures of hell. The leaping flames were like dancing devils. The darting sparks were thrown off by the burning people flailing about. She heard their muffled screams from deep inside the fire; voices struggling to be heard in the furious crackling fire.

She was startled by her mother's voice.

"Tell us more about school, Neo," Evelyn said.

"I told you everything in my letters."

"Tell us more about the trip," Evelyn said, "You traveled at night when you went."

"Well, this time I saw the Orange Free State," Neo said. "There's nothing much to see. It's mostly farms. I didn't like it."

"How were the exams?" Evelyn said.

"Good," Neo said. "They said the reports will be mailed in two weeks. Know what the best thing is? On Sunday mornings, we don't go to the small chapel at the school. Instead we go to big St. Paul, the big Methodist church in Thaba 'Nchu. We march three miles to church in three lines to the sound of drums. The bugle sounds part of the way and its so nice. The sound of our feet on the road is rythmic and after a while it's like something is making your feet walk and you're not exerting yourself. The people wave and cheer us and we feel proud. I like going to church there."

"Yes, I've heard it's a beautiful church," Evelyn said. "That is Reverend Senne's church?"

Neo nodded. "He cries when he preaches," she said. "But we are used to it now. I like his sermons."

"You don't play any sports?" Evelyn asked.

"Nothing organized," Neo said. "But on Saturdays, a group of us from my class play basketball."

"That's good," Evelyn said. "I thought you weren't playing anything at all."

"I was able to get out of the compulsory tryouts for track." Neo laughed. "Know how I did it? I showed the teacher my flat feet and told him I've always been exempted because my feet hurt. I don't know what he'll say when he sees me playing tennis next term."

"Neo," Edward said. "Lying to a teacher?"

"Well," Neo said. "I'm not lying. I've got flat feet, right Mummy?"

Evelyn nodded her head and chuckled.

"I always come in last," Neo said. "The purpose is to find out who can run fast, and I know I can't. So why waste anybody's time?"

Edward smiled and shook his head. "Neo, you know that's not the point."

Neo smiled. "At sports tryouts, everybody says they can't believe I can't run because Pitso was the best mile runner Moroka ever had. He'd have been champion if blacks were allowed to represent the country. Teacher Modupi said he would've been the national champion if this was a normal country and these whites weren't so selfish. He said Pitso just glided over the earth like he didn't even touch the ground."

"Don't worry," Pitso said. "All that's going to change. Blacks will be running one day."

"Is it true the police beat them everyday?" Neo asked, suddenly changing the subject. "Is it true they didn't let you see Tiro while he was detained because the boys were all bleeding and broken?"

Evelyn said, "Where did you hear that?"

"At school, some of the kids said that was what happened to detainees, political ones," Neo said. "They said, some nights, the police took them to Hartebeespoort Dam and put them in big sacks and dipped them in cold water until they almost drowned."

Silence. Edward looked away.

The idea of beatings, Neo could handle. But, the idea of being dipped in water, tied her stomach in knots. It caused her to have more drowning dreams. The dreams were getting worse.

"Well, they did beat them up some," Evelyn said and looked at Edward. "But now, your brother is healthy. He survived, and that's what's important. The beatings are over because they are going to be seen in court."

Edward took off his glasses, and wiped them with a white handkerchief, then pressed the ridges of his nose between his fingers. "We should go to bed early today."

That night in bed, Neo tried different sleeping positions, on her stomach, left side, right side, on her back with knees bent and feet flat, and on her back with legs straight. Nothing seemed to work.

The furniture in her room had been rearranged, and she thought that might be the problem. She got up and dragged her bed around and settled it against the wall. Finally she fell asleep.

She dreamed she was playing with her friends in the street. The sun suddenly set, and it became very dark. She ran towards home but she couldn't see anything. Suddenly, she fell into water. She heard a thrashing sound and someone screamed, "Mamogashwa! Mamogashwa!" Neo kicked wildly, and clutched a tree stump by the bank of the river. Something touched her.

She screamed. "Koko!" and woke up. She stretched her arm and quickly turned on the light and sat up on the bed. She propped up the pillows against the headboard and went back to sleep sitting up. That way she'd be ready to run in her dreams.

CHAPTER 8

Court-Day One

Evelyn, Edward, Pitso, Kagiso, and Neo drove to court that morning. They were quiet, as though they were in a funeral procession. As they crossed the bridge over the train tracks and left Melodi behind, Evelyn felt as though they were going to a foreign hostile country, enemy territory, the devil's place. She felt uncertain whether they would come back alive.

This was really the trial of her life. She would make sure she stayed strong for her family. She wouldn't allow her children to be destroyed. If anybody thought they'd see her tears, well, they'd be disappointed. Not that she was the sort to cry, but she made a special resolution not to cry during this trying period. Her life was threatening to unravel; she could not afford any weakness.

They drove through town on Church Street, the main street, and in the center of town turned left on Paul Kruger Square. The gray twenty-foot statue towered high in the center. Paul Kruger sat high on a granite pedestal, and his big feet rested on a platform below. He wore a hat and held a walking stick. His face was serious as he looked East at the town like a Lord surveying his land.

"That's Paul Kruger," Neo said, as though she were seeing it for the first time.

"Yes," Evelyn said.

"It's good to see that the birds are peeing on his thick head," Pitso said.

"He's a piss-head," Neo said and then laughed nervously.

Nobody laughed with her. Edward didn't react, but Evelyn smiled. She was glad Neo, unlike the others, didn't seem to appreciate the danger of her imprisoned brother. She knew Neo got depressed, but then she'd snap out of it and crack a sarcastic joke.

"He was the one who was president of the Transvaal Republic when gold was discovered," Neo said. "And, he tried to keep the gold mines for the Afrikaners. But the English wouldn't let him. We did that history in Standard Six."

"That's right," Evelyn said.

"Mummy," Neo began. "You know what else he did?"

"What?"

"He drank tea out of a saucer when he visited England and met with the Queen, and the English laughed at him and thought he was crude like all the Afrikaners." Neo laughed hysterically.

Edward shook his head. "Neo, where do you get these things?"

"School," Neo said. "Our teacher said never to write it down in an exam or anything official, because whites don't like it."

"You want to learn another white joke?" Kagiso, the Maru's second child, said.

"Tell me," Neo said.

"You know the one about white people and their Christianity," Kagiso said. "Europeans came to our country, and when they first arrived, they had only Bibles. They said, let's pray and by the time they said 'Amen' and Africans opened their eyes, the Europeans had grabbed all the land and cattle and the Africans were left holding the Bible."

Neo laughed. "I have to remember this one so I can tell it to my friends at school."

"And what's worse," Pitso added, wagging his finger, "within a few days of their arrival they were accusing Xhosas of stealing their cattle, as though they came here with anything—the thieves!"

They stopped at a red light.

Kagiso pointed to a gray building. "Do you see that building?" he asked. "That's Compol Building. That's where Tiro was detained during that period when Mummy and Ntate couldn't see him."

"Is that where they beat them up?" Neo asked.

"Yes," Kagiso said.

Silence. Edward cleared his throat.

Neo asked, "Is that where the Special Branch threw that black man out a ninth floor window and claimed he committed suicide?"

The incident had happened while Neo was at school. Evelyn had been glad she wasn't around to grow scared for Tiro's life. She was surprised Neo knew about the horrible death.

"Well, they are still investigating." Even though Edward was convinced like everybody else that it was a murder, he said this just so Neo wouldn't get scared and think her brother would be killed by the security police.

"Yes, they killed that man, those dogs," Evelyn said. "The inquest was just a sham." Evelyn slightly regretted saying this, since she knew what her husband was trying to do. She'd never forget the impact of that so-called suicide the day it was announced. Edward couldn't sleep a wink that night, he was so totally terrified.

"We are almost there now," Edward said. "Just around the corner."

They turned onto Skinner Street and parked at a parking garage near the court.

The Supreme court building was red brick with five big columns in front and a long set of stairs. It threw a huge cold shadow over the street.

White police swarmed all over, some with leashes restraining German Shepherds with huge ears and wide mouths.

"Scary dogs," Neo said.

"They look like their owners," Pitso said.

"Neo, you have to be very careful," Evelyn said. "You stay close to me at all times. They are dying to set their vicious dogs on people."

"So many photographers," Neo observed.

"Journalists." Kagiso said.

"Some of them definitely police photographers," Pitso said, "Special Branch pigs mingling too."

Flash bulbs clicked around the Marus as photographers took pictures as they approached the court.

A man came over and greeted Edward and Evelyn. "We don't know each other, but my son, Chris Tulo, was in Tiro's class." The man said, "Our prayers are with you and Tiro."

A woman in a black and green hat came to greet them. "Mistress," she said facing Evelyn. "I'm Maggie's mother, Maggie in your Wayfarer group. Remember, she was in the group you took camping last year?"

"Oh, yes, of course I know Maggie," Evelyn said smiling.

Maggie's mother wiped a tear with the back of her hand. "We are so sorry. You are not alone," she said, and pointed. "Your girls are here to support you. There's Maggie over there."

Evelyn looked in that direction, but could not distinguish people in that large crowd. "Thank you."

A boy in an orange and green soccer uniform also pushed through to greet them. "The football team is all here, Mistress."

Various people, even the ones the Marus did not recognize, came to greet them and to offer their support.

A reporter asked a question. "I'm John Bridges from the *Rand Daily Mail*. Can you tell us what you think about all this, your son's trial?"

Edward said, "We don't have any comment except to say it's a sad day."

Evelyn pulled Edward gently by the hand, while holding Neo with the other one.

A short distance away, a group of young people sang. "This is our land, and we'll take it whether you like it or not. Nothing is going to stop us."

Peter, Edward's nephew pushed through the crowd. "Uncle, Auntie," Peter said. "We can take comfort in the fact that the whole community is with us. There are people even from Johannesburg, and of course, our old Kilnerton friends are here. There are other church people too."

Peter stated the obvious. He talked too much even when he had nothing to say. It irritated Evelyn.

"Nice to see you, nephew," Edward said. "We don't see much of you these days."

"You know, Uncle," Peter said. "I've been interviewing for that inspector's position. I've been busy, very busy. Sorry."

"I haven't heard about that," Evelyn said.

"Eh, thought I mentioned it, eh," Peter stammered.

"Good luck," Evelyn said.

"We'll talk about that another time, Auntie," Peter said. "There are more important things going on for our family. Jobs are nothing."

His words surprised Evelyn and Edward. Usually people became inspectors after having been principal for at least a few years. Peter wasn't a principal and didn't have the usual amount of teaching experience. But Evelyn knew never to trust Peter. Anyway, it was good to see that even unreliable, unpredictable people like Peter, knew that families stood together at times like these.

"This weather is strange, uncle," Peter said.

"Rain in June is unusual," Edward said.

"I hope it doesn't rain. Just washed my car this morning." Peter said.

Even though it was cool Peter was sweating. With characteristic showmanship, he pulled out his big white handkerchief, shook it open vigorously, and wiped his face. Evelyn noted his nervousness and attributed it to fear of what might happen if things got out of hand.

A tall man with glasses extended his hand to greet Edward, then Evelyn. "Pleased to meet you, even though we wish it was under happier circumstances. I'm Mareka, Matthew's father, the one who fled to Botswana."

"Oh yes," Edward said. "We thank God your son escaped before they could get him."

Evelyn extended her hand to the short woman with Mr. Mareka. "Is this Matthew's mother?" Evelyn asked.

"No, this is my sister. My wife said to give you her love and to tell you her prayers are with you," Mr. Mareka said. "She's in the hospital, heart trouble, otherwise she'd definitely be here."

"My God," Evelyn said. "What they've put us through, these devils. These are hard times, but things will pass. The sun will rise."

"What can we say?" Mr. Mareka said.

"All this will come to an end. You know what they say, *se se sa feleng se a thlola,*"Evelyn said. "Everything must come to an end."

"That is for sure," the woman with Mr. Mareka said.

"Tell Matthew's mother we are thinking of her," Evelyn said. "Don't worry, it'll be all right."

The women were well-dressed, church style. They wore hats, all types, pill box, wide brimmed. One of the women said, "This is a crucifixion; at least Jesus was thirty years old."

"Such a small child," the woman in the yellow felt hat added.

Many were teachers, which made it easier to come since school was closed for vacation. They were a close-knit group, the 'Kilnerton people' as they still liked to call themselves.

It started to rain, a cold rain, not the rain that is a blessing. It was a bad omen.

The supreme court building was huge inside, with very high ceilings and windows letting in weak light from the gray sky.

They filed into the courtroom and people scrambled to find seats. A woman shouted as the Marus entered court. "You are not alone! Tiro is not the only one on trial. All our children are on trial!"

Evelyn glanced in the direction of the voice. She smiled and waved to acknowledge the support. She felt a strange blend of pain and pride. The seats in the public gallery were soon taken and many were refused entry.

The press gallery was full and reporters spilled into the seats reserved for regular spectators, causing people to grumble. The only white spectators were reporters, with a few other white people representing organizations like the Race Institute and Human Rights Association.

Outside, there was shouting. "You are dogs, just like your dogs." Women swore at the police and their dogs.

A tall young woman in knee-high boots and hair braided in thin cornrows shouted, "Our men are on trial."

"There's Tiro," Neo whispered, as though surprised to see him. They all waved. Neo blew him a kiss.

His shaved head made him resemble his father even more. Tiro was neatly dressed in a light blue shirt and a navy jacket. Some people raised the clenched fist salute and referring to the land said,"*Elethu*, It is ours." Some shouted, "*Amandla*! Power" Some boys in soccer uniforms shouted "Pro!", Tiro's football name.

Evelyn locked her gaze on Tiro to see if there were any marks on his face. He looked thinner, but strong. The skin of his face was smooth. His ears, which always looked as though he was on alert, stood out even more on his shaved head. His eyes had their usual vigilance.

Tiro looked fit, like the soccer player that he had been, looking even younger than his seventeen years.

All the suppressed tears boiled inside Evelyn's chest; she took in a deep breath to cool the fire inside.

"All rise!" the court clerk ordered. "Justice Blackwell presiding."

The white judge's black robe seemed to fill the whole place like the minister's robe at church. He walked swiftly, took his seat and surveyed the court through his shimmering gold-rimmed eye glasses that stood out against his high shiny forehead.

Tiro sat upright, alert like a student, listening attentively in class. His palms rested on his thighs. He didn't look as pained as Evelyn expected. The corners of his mouth were raised very slightly, the way one would, out of politeness, or like watching a performance by mediocre clowns. He seemed confident, probably a sign of his certainty about the righteousness of his cause. It was the kind of confidence and certainty that only a young person could possess, Evelyn knew. Some might say he was too young to understand the gravity of his case.

The prosecutor, Mr. Snyman, a red-haired white man of medium height, came forward. He spoke in a thick Afrikaner accent. "The accused is charged with the following: One, High Treason, threatening to overthrow the State. Two, under the Sabotage Act, attempted sabotage. Three, under the Prevention of Communism Act, advancing the aims of Communism. Four, under the Banned Organizations Act, belonging to an outlawed organization, and advancing the aims of said organization."

The prosecutor continued, alledging Tiro conspired to kill the principal, Mr. Louw, and the other white teachers. He also charged Tiro planned to burn down the school buildings. The prosecutor finally paused to let the information sink in.

Then he continued. "The state will show that this was a carefully-made plan, where the defendant set a date, procured weapons, and even assigned different tasks to various people."

"The defendant and the group he led, plotted to kill their teachers at Hebron High School in cold blood. The attack was planned for April fourteenth," he said, then paused, sighed and looked at the judge. "Thanks to the diligent work of the police, the scheme was foiled at the last minute.

"The defendant and his group are members of a banned organization, the Movement, which planned to launch simultaneous attacks throughout the country on this date," the prosecutor continued. "They planned to overthrow the government and plunge the country into chaos. This was a well-orchestrated plot."

People gasped, and others whispered to each other. Evelyn straightened her back and sat up from the back of the bench. She wrinkled her brow. The Boers truly are evil, she thought. The prosecutor was enjoying himself. Evelyn wished she could slap the silly devilish smirk off his face. Her gentle child was being tormented. At home, Tiro was quiet and hard-working. She felt proud that her son was part of larger forces aiming to overthrow the government, but she feared greatly for his life in prison.

The judge leaned forward, rested his elbows and arms on the podium, interlocked his hands, and fixed his gaze firmly on the prosecutor.

"Pigs," someone whispered behind Evelyn.

The word 'innocent' jarred Evelyn. She never thought of white people as innocent.

Judge Blackwell looked at his watch. "The court will be in recess until eleven-thirty."

The judge rose, with his black robes trailing, and ambled towards his chambers.

Evelyn and Edward stayed inside. Pitso and Kagiso went outside to stretch their legs.

Neo stood and said, "I'll go out, to get fresh air."

"Why don't you stay with us?" Edward said. "It's chilly outside."

"But I have to go to the toilet." Neo said.

Evelyn smiled. Neo always knew how to get around restrictions. She probably knew that her father just wanted to keep an eye on her.

"O.K. come on, I'll go to the toilets with you," Evelyn said to Neo.

When the court resumed, the prosecutor called his first witness, John Mpofu. John rose slowly, scratched his bald head and edged into the witness stand gingerly as though a bomb were planted there and might explode if he stepped carelessly. He seized the teak arm rests, and eased himself onto the seat. He sat with his shoulders hunched and head scrunched, as though he were trying to stuff it into his small body. He had a glazed look in his eyes like he was sleep-walking. His clothes looked too big and he scratched his jaw nervously

The months of detention showed on his gray face and puffed eyes. He'd been detained with Tiro and became a state witness. He was to stay in detention or 'protective custody' until the trial was over.

State witnesses were loathed by the black community, but this one, John, elicited more pity than hate. He was only nineteen years old, and had been in the same class with Tiro.

The prosecutor rose and with a great flourish, like a bull-fighter going into the ring with great confidence, he marched towards John.

"So, Mr. Mpofu, how long have you known the accused, Tiro Maru?"

"Since 1959, when we first entered Kilnerton High School."

"How well have you known him throughout this time?"

"Very well" John said, not looking at the gallery at all. He kept his gaze on the prosecutor. His head bent, like he was looking from under a rock.

"How well?" the prosecutor asked.

"We were always in the same class," John said, "and we also played on the soccer team together."

The trial felt like a dream to Evelyn. Her seventeen year old boy was in the Supreme Court, not the lowly magistrate's court. There was something majestic about this. The imposing building could be seen as a reflection not of the gravity of her son's situation, but as a reflection of his greatness. He was a young man, big enough to take on a great challenge, the freedom of his people. She still could not believe it.

The pain inside her heart was unbearable. It was like a raw open wound with gushing blood. But, she would not allow the blood to burst through her skin. She was going to sit upright and be strong. How could she do otherwise when her son was sitting upright with dignity? He was a real hero. She was going to give him strength by being strong herself. She adjusted her hat and looked at Tiro. He still sat strong, even though he was watching his friend betray him.

But Evelyn knew John had no choice. Still she couldn't see it as anything but betrayal even though she knew the police had broken him.

John was only trying to save his life. John's thin gray face, gray like a corpse, hung heavy, as though it was on the verge of dropping to the ground and revealing the bare bones. He was like a scared hare, face to face with a hunting dog. Unlike this pathetic miserable creature, her own son was a hero. Evelyn felt proud.

Mr. Snyman, the prosecutor, called Simon Zwane to the stand.

Simon sat in the witness box with bent head, rounded shoulders hunched to his ears, and hands clasped tightly together on his lap.

Mr. Snyman's face was relaxed, except for the corners of his mouth which were raised slightly in a smirk. He had one hand in his pocket, and strutted towards Simon.

Simon covered his mouth and coughed.

"Mr. Zwane, explain to the court how you first learned of the plans of the defendant," Mr. Snyman said and stepped back a few feet.

Simon raised his head a bit, and spoke slowly. He dragged his voice as though it took all his energy to talk. "The Sunday before Easter, I attended a meeting."

Mr. Snyman nodded slowly and took a step closer to Zwane. "Who chaired that meeting?"

"Tiro Maru."

"What happened at that meeting?"

"Tiro told the group the date of the attack had been fixed."

"And what was the date?"

"April eighth," Zwane said, softly.

"Describe to the court the plan and how it was to be carried out."

"The people from Hebron were to break into two groups. One group was to go to Lady Selbourne to fight, and the second group was to remain at school in Hebron. Tiro said the Hebron group's main task was to kill the white teachers at the college."

"Describe to the court what happened on the morning of April eight."

Simon shifted around in his seat. "On the morning of April eighth, I went to Garankuwa," Simon said, referring to a black township. "When I got there, I tried to persuade the others to give up the plan and to return to school with me…but they said we had to go on."

"Then, what happened?"

"Later, I met a group of men in the veld."

"What did the men have in their possession?" Mr. Snyman asked.

"Weapons," Mr. Zwane said and paused. "Clubs and pieces of piping."

Mr. Snyman asked the court to note the evidence of weapons. When he held up clubs, sticks and pieces of piping some people laughed, some of them quite loudly.

A man in the back blurted, "They call that weapons?"

People laughed.

Mr. Snyman shot a sharp glance towards the spectators, and then at the judge who banged his gavel and called for order. He threatened to throw out anybody who disrupted the proceedings of the court.

Mr. Snyman hitched up his pants and stared the witness. "What else?" he said.

"Peter Mampa and I were sent to cut telephone wires."

"That's all for now, your Honor," Mr. Snyman said and sat down.

The defense lawyer, Mr. Brecht, rose to cross-examine. He walked over to the witness stand slowly.

"Mr. Zwane, did you know the people you met at the meeting?"

"Yes."

"Were they your friends?"

"Yes."

"Had you met in the past as friends."

"Yes."

"Were there any other weapons besides the little clubs and sticks displayed by the prosecution?"

"No."

"You mean these little sticks and things were all the weapons that were going to overthrow the best armed government on the continent?" Mr. Brecht asked with fresh incredulity. He rolled his eyes in mock disbelief.

A few spectators chuckled.

"Mr. Zwane, was there any coercion by the police during your interrogation?"

Simon hung his head.

"Mr. Zwane, were you beaten by the police during your interrogation?"

Simon cleared his throat. "I was beaten many times," he said with a cracking voice. He rested his elbows on the stand and hid his face in his hands.

"Is that why you're saying these things against Tiro?"

Mr. Snyman shouted, "Objection, your honor."

Quickly, Mr. Brecht said, "No further questions, your honor."

"The court will adjourn for lunch." the judge said.

Evelyn felt sorry for Simon. She remembered the previous week's reports about the death of a young man who had been detained at Compol Building where Tiro and his friends were. Everybody knew that the police explanation of the boy's death had been a lie. The boy had not slipped on a bar of soap, but had been murdered.

Thank God Tiro survived the torture. This was a weak case. But the courts were not fair. If convicted, Tiro would serve his prison term, come out and continue with his life, Evelyn thought. The sentence would be short. He was still young. Who knows, black people might get free before he even completed his sentence.

After lunch the prosecutor called Jonathan Mzami, a young man Evelyn did not know.

"At the meeting Tiro Maru made a speech," Jonathan said.

"What did he say in the speech?" Mr. Snyman asked.

"He said we had to be prepared for April eighth and that he would direct all operations."

"What happened when the time came?"

"On April seventh, I was sent to buy a gallon of petrol. I later heard that the petrol was to set fire to the houses of the three white men. Tiro Maru sent some of the accused to collect weapons such as sticks and lengths of iron piping. He instructed others to pour petrol into three bottles, one for each house."

"Who directed all this activity?"

"Tiro Maru gave all the instructions."

Mr. Brecht rose to cross-examine.

"Mr. Mzami did you make your statements to the police freely?"

"No," Jonathan said and looked down.

"Why?"

"Every time I said something they did not like, the police beat me and said I was talking nonsense," Jonathan said and then added quickly, "But this did not make me change my statements at all." He wiggled around in his chair as though it were hot.

Mumbling and hissing started in the gallery. The judge banged his gavel and called for order.

"When did you first get to know Tiro?" Mr. Brecht asked him.

"I heard the name Tiro for the first time from the police," He said, "I do not know him."

Spectators cried out, then hushed to whispers.

"All lies!" a woman at the back shouted.

Tiro smiled. The attorneys at the prosecutor's table shifted in their seats and shuffled papers. The prosecutor, his mouth tight as though he was trying hard not to blurt something out focused his intense eyes on Jonathan who covered his eyes with his hand.

Later, another state witness, Alfred Matthews, walked towards the stand. He looked surprisingly well for someone who had been incarcerated. His skin had a healthy shine to it and he was a little overweight. His faced was relaxed and he seemed at ease as though this was a job he was used to doing. He sat upright in the chair.

"I attended the April seventh meeting and Tiro was there saying there was going to be a general uprising the following day on the eighth." He spoke very formally as though rehearsed. "Various tasks were assigned, and some students were chosen to take the cars of the three white teachers. Tiro told us we had to carry out all instructions in all circumstances, and if we did not, he threatened the organization would send a special task force to deal with us. I realized this was a suicide mission. I was also not sure what would happen if we failed to carry out instructions. I volunteered to drive one of the cars, even though I did not know how to drive. It was my intention to tell them at the last minute that I could not drive and I hoped this would derail the plan."

"Thank you," Mr. Snyman said. "Your witness"

Mr. Brecht cross-examined. "What did you think the petrol was for?"

"When I poured the petrol into three bottles I thought it was for the cars and not to burn houses," Alfred said.

"How old are you, Mr. Matthews?"

"Twenty."

"And, you want the court to believe this seventeen-year-old was your leader?" He looked at Snyman. "No further questions."

The court adjourned.

It broke Evelyn's heart to see her son surrounded by police, going down the stairs into the hole. Neo cried and Edward put his arm around her shaking shoulders.

Outside, the family waited. The van carrying Tiro to take him to the high security jail passed. The tight wire mesh on the small windows made it impossible to distinguish his features. He was just a shadow without much definition. Just a shape, as though he was fading out of life already. Evelyn felt like she was losing her child, he was disppearing in so many ways.

The van carrying him sped away.

A group of young people sang "This burden you're carrying is for my land". They danced and stomped their right feet when they said, "land". Others joined in. Edward's eyes were deep red and Evelyn knew he was crying without tears.

"My son," Edward whispered.

"It will be all right my dear," Evelyn said and took his arm.

Like sleepwalkers, they moved to the car. A thin, but sharp winter wind blew through them.

"It's cold," Edward said.

Evelyn said, "It's not warming up today."

On the drive home, they remained quiet until they left the center of town.

"He looked good," Evelyn finally said.

"He's thin," Neo observed.

"Only a little," Evelyn said, softly.

Edward braked hard as the light changed to red and they were thrown forward.

"Sorry," he said.

"Boy," Pitso said, "I can't believe they broke John. God knows what they must do to them."

"I feel sorry for him," Edward said. "You could see he was deeply ashamed and he's going to be a pariah forever, poor thing."

"Sorry for him!" Evelyn exclaimed. "I feel sorry for my son! he's the one going to prison if he's found guilty."

No one spoke for a while; they all felt Evelyn's anger.

"It's not that I don't feel sorry for him," Evelyn continued, "My child I know would rather die than turn State Witness. He's bold."

"Maybe it's just as well he was the leader," Pitso said. "Had he been one they needed as state witness, he would have been hard to break. They would have killed him."

"Let's just thank God he survived the interrogations," Edward said.

"So, John's a sell-out?" Neo asked.

"Not quite," Kagiso said. "Sellouts betray others willingly. John was probably coerced. He's not the type to double cross on his own."

"God knows what they are going to do to Simon for saying he was beaten," Pitso said.

"Oh, God," Evelyn said. "Monsters."

Edward stepped on the accelerator harder.

"This judge worries me," Evelyn said. "It's as though he's bored. He's hard to read."

Pitso raised his voice. "He's typical English. They bite with a smile. Can't stand them. Afrikaners don't pretend to be anything other than brutes."

"I hope he's not going to use my brother to prove he's just as tough as any Afrikaner." Kagiso said.

"It's true," Pitso said. "An Afrikaner is a man with rotten principles, all of which he's prepared to die for. An English man is a man with many lofty principles, none of which he's prepared to die for."

Neo pounded the air with a clenched fist and shouted, "Pigs, snakes, dogs, all Whites."

"Neo!" Edward said.

"All whites are satans!" She said, ignoring her father.

"That's not true," Edward said. He slowed down and changed to a lower gear to turn towards Melodi. "There are some nice ones who are prepared to fight alongside people for freedom."

"Yea, all four of them." Pitso added.

"Pitso, you're not helping your sister," Edward said.

"Ntate, the English are mean and stingy and count food." Neo said.

Pitso and Kagiso chuckled.

Evelyn smiled. "Now, Neo, how do you know that. You've never been in an English home."

Neo laughed.

After they got home, they sat in the kitchen, warmed and infused with the smell of fried onions and tomatoes. Koko stood against the wall, between the coal stove and the electric stove. With her left hand, she propped herself against the electric one, which was turned off. In the winter, they liked to use the cast iron coal stove because it heated the house too…but today they were all still chilled to the bone.

CHAPTER 9

Fafung

Evelyn and Edward decided they had to visit Edward's mother in Fafung. They were worried about how she was taking the news about Tiro since she had just recovered from a serious bout of pneumonia. Koko Sarah, as they called her to differentiate her from Koko, Evelyn's mother, had a special warm feeling for Tiro since his middle name, Selepe, was her husband's name. Evelyn knew seeing the other children would make Koko Sarah happy too.

The Marus left around four in the morning, since they intended to return the same day. The next day, Sunday, was a special service for youth and they did not want the children to miss it.

Evelyn had Pitso and Kagiso pack a lot of food in the trunk; big bags of sugar, rice, flour, mealie-meal, dried beans, and rusks. They also packed big boxes of soap and other washing and cleaning supplies, to help Koko Sarah since she took care of six of her grandchildren.

It would still be hours before the sun rose and it was cold outside. The street light threw a weak amber glow. When they were ready to leave, Neo jumped in the back seat and sat in the middle.

"You are seating in the back today?" Kagiso asked.

"Yes," Neo replied.

"But you always sit in front," Pitso said

"Not anymore. I'm big and I'm not going to sit in front like I'm a child," Neo said.

"In the front, you can see better," Pitso said.

"No." Neo shook her head.

"Maybe you should go to the front," Kagiso said.

"I'm not going," Neo said

"Neo you are wasting time," Pitso said.

"There's room, I'm sitting in Tiro's place," Neo said. "When he comes back, then I'll go to the front."

They were silent for a moment.

Pitso sighed deeply. "If you're going to sit back here with us," Pitso began, "then, you're going to have to stop fidgeting. Sit still like an adult. Otherwise you go to the front."

Finally Edward started the car and they began to move.

They were silent. It was their first family trip without Tiro and they were not whole.

Evelyn threw the green and red blanket with thick tussles at its end, into the back and Neo covered herself.

An hour into the trip they left the tarred road and turned right onto a wide dirt road. They drove for thirty minutes until they were behind a truck that left a thick cloud of dust in front of them. They passed the truck and drove for an hour through farm country. There were no houses or buildings next to the road—just bare trees, dead shrubs and burnt grass. In some parts, there were fences and in some, the land was just open as though it was free for the taking.

Two hours into the trip Edward parked on the side of the road, got out, and they all ate Gouda cheese sandwiches with tea and milk.

Neo took one bite, kept it in her mouth, and looked at the mountain in the distance.

"Neo," Edward said.

She was startled, as though she'd been sleeping. "Yes, Ntate, what?" Her eyes were wide and wild as though she was ready to run.

"You are very far," Evelyn said. "What are you thinking."

"Nothing," Neo said, and took a long deep breath. She looked at the sandwich in her hand. "I don't like this cheese."

"You like Gouda," Evelyn said. "That's your favorite."

Neo looked at her father. "Do they give them food in prison?"

"Yes," Edward said. "Maybe not things like cheese, but regular food certainly."

"Tiro likes meat," Neo said. "I heard they only give them porridge with a little stinky watery Kupugani soup."

"You saw Tiro," Evelyn said. "He looks healthy."

"He's thin." Neo sucked her cheeks in, exaggerating.

Kagiso took out an orange from the basket and gave it to Neo. "Here, these are very sweet, from Zebediela."

Neo rolled the orange between her hands. "Remember, Mummy, how in the paper last year a Boer beat the black man to death?"

They all ignored the question.

"Bananas are more filling," Pitso said. "Let's share this one."

Neo took the peeled half banana and ate it slowly.

Edward handed her a bottle of milk which she drank quickly.

"I think we should pack up and get going now." Evelyn said after they'd sat for thirty minutes.

"Maybe I'll sit in front now so I can see better," Neo said.

Evelyn smiled and nodded. She knew Neo was having a hard time with the trial.

They pushed down the road. A van passed by them, speeding and sending a small stone that smacked the windscreen. It made a small crack.

"It happens only when the car is new," Edward said. "It doesn't happen when the car is old."

"It's not as bad as the old days though, when one little stone shattered the whole windscreen," Evelyn said.

"That was terrible," Edward said. "The screen would have to be replaced".

They drove facing the sun. Outside, the monotonous gray landscape continued. When they came to a cattle gate, Kagiso started to get out to open the wooden gates. But, two little barefoot boys, in short pants and frayed oversized sweaters, opened the gates before Kagiso could get out of the car. Smiling broadly, the boys stood on either side of the road, and held the gates open. Edward stopped and gave them a few coins. This was the land of his childhood and a sentimental glow always warmed him there, no matter how tough things might be. They drove down the dirt road and turned onto a one lane road with a patch of grass in the center.

"We are in Fafung," Edward said.

"Bultfontein," Neo said. "That's the official name, right?"

"We are going to change these names," Pitso started, "back to their original names when we get our country back."

"After the revolution," Neo said.

Edward worried about how politically sensitive his children had become because of Tiro's imprisonment. He hoped it wouldn't harden them. The times were different. Young people weren't prepared to be patient anymore.

The car slowed to a crawl. A half mile later, the road became narrower. They passed a store with a van parked in front. Two white-haired men sat on the stoop. Edward waved and the men waved back.

On top of the building towered a huge billboard with a navy border, a black woman, wearing a white apron over a green dress and a wide smile with perfect shiny white teeth. She held a tray supporting a white porcelain teapot decorated with little blue flowers, a matching sugar basin and milk jug, a cup and saucer. On the right side of the ad was a gold box with 'Roses Tea' in bold red letters. Below the letters 'Roses Tea' was a picture of a single red rose with wide perfect petals. Below that at the bottom were the words, 'the tea that refreshes.'

Neo said, "So you walked to this store when you were a little boy, Ntate?"

"There was no store when we were growing up. The nearest store was in Boli," he said.

"You walked that far?" Neo askedd.

"Yes, and sometimes we used donkey carts."

A few yards down the road, they took the right fork.

"That's the road to the graveyard," Neo said, pointing to the left.

"Are we going to go there this time, Ntate?" Kagiso asked.

"I'm not sure we'll get a chance, since we aren't staying overnight."

"Maybe we'll go by ourselves, Kagiso," Pitso said.

"Yes," Kagiso said. "You know these days I think about Uncle Tshepo a lot."

"Who?" Neo askedd

"Your uncle Tshepo," Edward said.

"The white police killed him," Neo said, "I don't want them to kill my brother."

"Your brother is fine, Neo," Evelyn said.

"They kill them at night, put them in a sack, and drown them I heard. Sometimes, they put electricity on their private parts. Ooh!" Neo spoke quickly, saying the words in one breath, "If they kill him, I'll grab a white girl, pull her by her hair, kick her, and strangle her."

Neo kicked and threw punches in the air.

"Hey," Pitso said. "Careful, you'll hurt yourself. Save that energy for the whites."

Neo hit the dashboard, and pretended to pull hair.

Pitso and Kagiso laughed.

"Pitso, Kagiso," Edward said, softly, but firmly.

"You people should be ashamed laughing." Evelyn said. "Instead, you should help your sister. She's a child."

"I'm not a child," Neo said. "I can fight. I'll beat up the white girls."

"Remember, you don't believe in violence, Neo," Edward said.

"For white people, it's all right. They are thieves, and torturers, and murderers. I hate them."

"Neo, no." Edward sighed deeply. He slowed down to get around a stump on the road ane then continued. "Remember how you always agreed with Koko that it is not right to be hateful like Whites because then you go to Hell with them?"

"Whites are pigs, pigs, pigs," Neo said her voice rising with each "pig".

Pitso and Kagiso chuckled.

Evelyn looked at them disapprovingly. She didn't want her sons encouraging Neo. She was worried about Neo's acting out. Maybe Koko could help. Koko was more effective talking sense to Neo. Neo always believed what her grandmother said.

Evelyn did not blame Neo for feeling this way though but she did not want her to grow up troubled and to end up in prison too one day. She's quite a fighter. Maybe when the dust settles they should send her to the boarding school in Botswana to get her away from all this. Time in a different country would do her some good.

Evelyn's thoughts were interrupted.

"I think we'll make time to visit your uncle's grave later in the day," Edward said.

As they passed the cemetry Edward thought of his younger brother, Tshepo. He died as a young man. A dark shadow of sadness descended every time his name came up as if something catastrophic would happen if they talked about the details of his death.

Years ago in nineteen-forty-nine Tshepo and his friends had gone to Pretoria to find work. A group of white police-men beat them up for loitering. But Tshepo had blocked the blows effectively, thus making him look stubborn. So the police kicked him harder while he lay on the ground.

When the white men were gone the other young men carried Tshepo back to his home in Fafung. He died a few weeks later from internal injuries. The other young men had reported that when the white men had asked them who'd told them to come to town, one of the young men had pointed to Tshepo. According to the others, that was when the police started beating Tshepo harder.

"You know, Ntate," Pitso said. "It still makes me mad that my uncle was killed for nothing."

"It happened long ago," Edward said. "It's best to just forget. No use dredging up the past."

Even though Edward pretended to have put all this behind him, he always felt a twinge of pain each time he thought about it. He imagined his brother, Tshepo, lying on the ground, and being kicked like a soccer ball from one policeman to another. He could see the white men dribbling his body as though it were a soccer ball, and cheering as he rolled like a ball, down a steep ramp. Edward imagined him being beaten with clubs, until he lay lifeless, then, the white policemen with feet, as big as the feet on Paul Kruger's statue in the center of town, stomped his head with their boots.

The mental pictures became more painful as they mixed with images of the beatings of his son. He knew torture definitely took place during detention. He fought imagining Tiro being beaten with clubs, tortured with electricity, and lying lifeless on the cold cement floor. He didn't share these horrors with Evelyn.

The road narrowed to a strip of grass in the middle and two shallow furrows on each side. It was winter and the landscape was severe. The grass was brown grass and the land was covered with bare thorn trees. Here and there big trees like the mmopudi and morula which bore sweet wild fruit in the summer stood bare. The sky was a dull gray. The sun was weak.

Edward slowed the car to let a donkey cart squeeze into the side of the road, so that they could pass. The three men and two women in the cart waved and Edward waved back. Neo waved vigorously, almost into Edward's face.

They passed a big thatched-roof house, which belonged to Edward's sister, Mary.

"That's a mmopudi tree in front of Rakgadi Mary's house," Neo said.

"Do you remember the story about mmopudi and watermelon?" Edward said.

"Yes, we know it," Neo said. "I'll tell it! One hot summer day a lazy man lay on his back under a mmopudi tree, not far from a patch of huge watermelons. He looked up and saw the small mmopodi fruits. God must be stupid, he thought. Why else would he put small light fruits like mmopodi on such a big tall strong tree, and heavy fruits like watermelons on weak little trees so burdened they even collapse and crawl on the ground. Then the man fell asleep."

Pitso interrupted, "That's what happens…"

Neo pressed on. "A mmopudi fell on his nose and he got up and ran screaming like a crazy person because of the intense pain. When he calmed down, he looked up at the mmopodi tree. 'If this were a watermelon it would have killed me,' the man said. 'God is great.' "

"Excellent, Neo," Edward said, and everyone laughed.

Evelyn added, "You know what they say also, God beats even the wiliest witches."

"All the bad witches should go and bewitch all the whites, and then they can't bother us anymore and Tiro will come out of prison." Neo said.

No one responded.

Finally they arrived. The main house, the biggest of the buildings, was thatch-roofed, with a long covered stoop. On the other side of the courtyard were two smaller round houses, one thatch-roofed and one with a corrugated iron roof. Each had uncovered stoops in front.

Edward parked under the big Morula tree near the gate.

"It's a pity this is not morula time," Kagiso said, smacking is lips. "we'd make a morula drink."

"Not the alcoholic type, I hope!" Evelyn said, firmly.

They laughed.

"We're home, my children," Edward said.

"This is your home and our home is in Melodi," Neo said.

Edward shook his head. "No, this is your home too."

Pitso and Kagiso laughed. Evelyn smiled.

Edward's mother got up from the stoop to greet them. She wore a long brown dress that flowed down to her ankles and over the dress, was a blue print apron. A blue-striped scarf around her head leaned to one side. She walked with her arms behind her back, swaying slightly from side to side as she moved towards them. She kissed and hugged everybody, saying, "Oh, my children's children." She hugged and kissed Evelyn for a long time and said, "Evelyn, both the

Gods of the Marus and of the Manos will keep Tiro safe through this. They won't abandon their own." Her tears were flowing freely on her soft cheeks by the time she hugged and kissed Edward who was the last in line. "Remember, your son has your father's name, so he'll be okay. How can your father not protect him? Our ancestors are there watching. White people will not win."

Neo took her grandmother's hand as they walked towards the house. There were a lot of grandchildren and neighbors' children playing in the yard, so the greetings took a while.

Throughout the day, a steady stream of relatives and friends came to see them. Edward always took pride in explaining to his children their relationship to each relative. Sometimes, it was easy, like, "This is your grandmother's brother's daughter." But sometimes, it was more compli-cated like, "This is your cousin by marriage. Her aunt is married to your aunt's husband's cousin on his mother's side."

He was proud of his children, who always bore these vis-its with respect. They wore picture-perfect smiles as they were introduced. He felt grateful. His children came out all right.

One of Koko Sarah's neighbors, who came to greet the visitors, complimented the Marus. "You have such nice chil-dren. And well-behaved too. You wouldn't know they were city children."

He was always amused by the way they looked at Evelyn when they said these things, as though he had nothing to do with it. He and Evelyn exchanged glances and smiled when another old woman said, "Your girl is big now. She is the one who will fetch water for you."

They winced when Neo replied rather quickly, "I will not live where people have to fetch water far from their houses. I like the city."

The boys unloaded the groceries and took them inside. Evelyn pointed out the food to be kept separate for Edward's sister, Mary. They always helped her out, especially after her husband left her.

Edward and Evelyn had educated Peter, fully expecting that he'd then look after his mother. But Peter seldom did. He didn't visit much and when he did, he brought very little. They'd given up trying to get him to support his mother. Evelyn decided to support Mary, because as Evelyn said, "We might as well support her directly because when she runs out of food she'll go to mother anyway and then mother will run short."

Later Mary arrived. After she greeted them all she sat down and wiped the tears in her eyes. "I pray for my poor nephew, Tiro, everyday." She looked to the place a few feet away where their father's cattle kraal used to be.

After the sun went down and the guests had left, Edward called everybody to join him, outside in the yard. They congregated around a small rock that rested in the middle of what used to be his father's cattle kraal. As was the custom then, his father was buried in the center. The kraal was no longer there, but his father, Selepe, would always be there and the little rock marked the spot.

Edward needed his father very badly at this time. Wherever his father was, Edward believed he could hear the story. And since Tiro was the son who was keeping the old man's name alive, it could only help.

Edward fixed his gaze on the rock. "We've brought the children to see you, Father. As you know, one of them, your name-sake Selepe is not here with us." Edward thought to use the name Selepe over Tiro to mark the close connection. "He is in prison," Edward continued. "We know you are watching over him. Otherwise, he would not have survived the interrogations. We know you stayed with him during the long periods of solitary confinement."

As he spoke, his mother sobbed. Edward suspected it was not just for Tiro, but that the speech was dredging up painful memories of her own son, Tshepo. The cruel irony was that Tshepo's murder took place just a stone's throw away from the same Compol building where Tiro was detained.

Edward paused. He cleared his throat and then continued. "These are difficult times for the family, but we know your God and the God of our ancestors is always with us."

His sister Mary sobbed. Evelyn just cleared her throat. She didn't cry easily, especially when things were tough. She just got tougher.

The family stood silent for a few minutes. Finally, Edward extended his hand towards his mother who gave him the small gourd with homemade sorghum beer. Edward poured the beer on the ground next to the rock. The strong, sweet, sour smell of the beer wafted up into the cold winter air.

With slow steps, they went back into the house.

Edward's mother wiped her tears.

"Mother," Evelyn said. "Don't worry, he's going to be fine. The trial has started and the interrogation phase is now over."

"My poor grandchild," Edward's mother said. "I hope our ancestors don't abandon the child now."

"It's a pity we can't stay the night," Evelyn said.

They said their good-byes, hugging and kissing more desperately than earlier.

By the time they were finally ready to leave it was nine o'clock and it was pitch dark. There were no stars. They drove in silence as they passed the little store, and turned left onto the big dirt road. Suddenly, Edward braked.

"What was that, my dear?" Evelyn asked, noticing a dark outline on the road.

"I'm not sure," Edward said. "it looks like a hare."

"Did we hit it?" Neo asked.

"No."

They were quiet most of the way. Edward liked that; it made it easier for him to concentrate on the road. Driving at night on dirt roads with no street lights was difficult. Hitting a big animal like a springbok could wipe out a car's front, and Edward wanted no more tragedies for his family.

CHAPTER 10

Sunday-Church
—Youth Day

Edward started Sunday as usual by walking to buy the Sunday Times half a mile away at the bus and taxi station. Edward gave him exact change plus a tip. As Edward approached, the paper boy smiled, handed him the paper, took the money with cupped hands as a sign of respect. Without counting the money, he dropped it in the pocket of his blue denim apron. "Thank you teacher," he said respectfully.

When Edward returned home, he scanned. On this Sunday, the big headlines on the front page screamed "FREE STATE FARMERS CHARGED UNDER IMMORALITY ACT-ONE COMMITS SUICIDE." Underneath the caption was a big picture of two sad-looking black women with seven children of mixed parentage huddled around. Edward shook his head. How terrible. It was ironic that these farmers were the most backward and strongest supporters of the government. This was a crazy world.

The article next to it had the headline: MINISTER OF JUSTICE PROMISES TO CRACK DOWN HARD ON COMMUNISTS AND TERRORISTS. He read the article and trembled, fearful for his poor son's fate. Anybody who was against Apartheid was either a Communist or a terrorist.

Edward put the paper down on the kitchen table, and went outside to wash the car. He needed to get his mind off these fears.

He washed the car. It was good exercise. Besides, children, even the older ones, were not thorough. They didn't use enough water or rinse the cloths well. They tended to scratch the car too. A clean unscratched car helped when it came time for a trade-in.

Evelyn hoed the garden over the fence, next to where Edward was washing the car. He was glad she didn't just admire a beautiful garden but enjoyed tending it herself. He wasn't much for gardening. It was strange when he considered that he was the one who grew up working on a farm. In Fafung, his family grew most of their food, and it sure wasn't easy.

He gave the car a good rinse with the hose to remove dust before following up with a soapy cloth. He started on top, and then he looked up when he heard a woman's voice.

"*Saubona* Mistress," Ma-Malambane, George's mother said,

Evelyn straightened up. "*Yebo*, Ma-George"

"Mistress," Ma-Malambane said, adjusting her brown wool cap. "You're always working hard. So many boys, you shouldn't have to work in the garden."

"They're inside cooking and cleaning," Evelyn said.

Ma-Malambane laughed. "Your boys are really nice. They're so big, but they still help in the house. You're lucky."

Evelyn laughed. "They're not doing me a favor. They're cooking for themselves. They eat in this house too."

"But you know how when they reach this age, they think they're men," Ma-Malambane said.

"Not in my house. Their father is the man of this house. They'll be men in their own houses."

The two women laughed heartily.

"Really, serious, Mistress," Ma-Malambane said, "We're always talking about how nice your children are. Not spoiled like the children of the other teachers."

"There's no trick really," Evelyn said. "If you start early, they grow up used to doing it."

"You're right, we treat our boys, even small ones, as though they are men and not children. But you teach them, and when they grow, their friends in the street laugh at them and tell them they're doing women's work."

"They're free to go and be men in their own houses," Evelyn said, firmly.

Ma-Malambane laughed and continued on her way.

Edward was proud of his wife. But, she could be difficult at times. She really had a lot to do with how well their children turned out. Her strong hand helped. It was good for Neo, who would've otherwise been stuck waiting on her brothers.

He remembered before they had children, Evelyn used to say she wouldn't let her daughters wait on their brothers the way she had to. Evelyn was an only girl. She was going to make sure her daughters had their own careers, so they wouldn't be anybody's servant.

Evelyn pulled dead carnations.

Neo joined her mother at the garden. "I'm tired, Mummy,"

"Nightmares again?" Evelyn asked.

"Yes, but it's not the nightmares that make me tired this time."

"Couldn't fall asleep?" Evelyn said. "It's hard when you're too tired sometimes. We got back too late yesterday. Later, you should take a very long nap."

"No no, no," Neo said, "it wasn't that."

"What was it?"

"Things."

"What things?"

"I know *Tikoloshe* is a myth, but last night there was something walking on the roof. It walked slowly, and when I raised my head from the pillow to listen carefully, it stopped. Then when I put my head down, it walked on the roof again."

"Did you turn on the light?"

"Yes, but at first I was afraid to stick my hand from under the blanket. I stuck it out quickly and knocked the bed-lamp off so I covered myself and lay there for a few minutes. Then, I jumped up quickly turned on the big light. But you know how even though there is no such thing as *Tikoloshe*," Neo paused, barely taking a breath. "They say it has mysterious powers and it can see through the roof and come in and slap you if you don't keep quiet. Or if he smells that you are planning to turn on the light."

Evelyn put the small gardening fork down. "You did well to turn the light on. You know what Koko always says, 'light will always defeat darkness.'"

"I guess so," Neo said. "The thing went away after I turned the light on."

"Maybe it was a cat or something like that," Evelyn said. "Nothing to worry about. You're safe."

Tikoloshe was one of those myths that children grew up with. It was a creature, a short man, owned by a witch who used him to prowl at night. He liked darkness and would dance on roofs. But The Marus always taught their children that these were just myths. So Evelyn was surprised that after all these years, Neo was thinking about these tales again. This trial was really affecting Neo. She and Edward would have to pay extra attention to their daughter so she didn't suffer too much through all this. It was a pity. It would've been better if the trial had taken place while school was in session.

"Did you remember to pray last night?" Evelyn asked.

"No, I fell asleep," Neo said.

"Remember how you got rid of the Mamogashwa and water nightmares for a while by praying the special prayer Koko gave you?" Evelyn said.

Neo didn't say anything.

Edward came over to the fence and wrung his drying cloth. "Looks like there's a good conversation here I won't disturb."

"Ntate, don't go," Neo said. "Remember the silly myth which we used to believe when we were children? At night, the witches come and take you and ride you like a horse while they're doing their errands. Then, when you wake up, you're tired and you don't know you've been ridden the whole night."

"Yes," Edward said. "It's just an old superstition."

Neo laughed, a strained, exaggerated laugh. "Yes, it's so silly! I don't see why people believe such stupid things!"

"These are the kind of stories people made up around the fire long ago, and then they were passed on to scare children," Evelyn said.

"But, Mummy. Many adults believe these things too," Neo said.

Evelyn looked at Edward.

"Remember the saying that God can defeat witches?" Evelyn said.

"That's what Koko used to say," Neo said.

Evelyn excused herself and went into the kitchen to see how the cooking was going. She'd let Edward talk to Neo about this. He liked to teach his children about psychology anyway. Neo adored her father, and with everybody so busy, she probably didn't see as much of him as she would have liked to. It was good to give them every chance to be together.

Edward looked up when he heard the noisy gate open. It was his nephew Peter. After opening the gate, Peter pulled his car into the driveway. It was a green Plymouth with 'fish tails' and it appeared ready to take off and fly. Since he bought the car a month before, Peter no longer parked in the street like everybody. He pulled it into the yard even if he was just staying a few minutes.

The children named the car the 'Flying Squad.' Peter liked that.

"Come in, *Motlogolo*," Edward said to his nephew. "Your cousins are in the kitchen."

"Malome, how are you," Peter greeted his uncle.

They went into the kitchen where Pitso was shucking peas and Kagiso mashing potatoes. Peter went straight for the fruit bowl, grabbed a green pear and bit into it immediately.

"You should wash it," Edward said. "There's dust on the fruit."

"Dust doesn't kill uncle," Peter said.

"Here's a chair, sit down," Edward said.

"No, thanks," Noga said, "I'm not staying, have to do some things before church."

Peter glanced at the paper on the table. "Another removal?"

"I can't wait for the revolution to come," Pitso said. "Then, we can throw these bastards into the ocean and send them swimming to wherever they came from."

"This Bantustan business is really getting serious," Peter said. "Maybe it's just as well, since there's no hope we'll ever defeat the whites. They've got this place sewed up. We might as well cooperate and develop the Bantustans where at least we can have some power."

"You're damn crazy," Pitso said. "You call dust-bowl dumping grounds places to develop? Man, this whole country is ours, not just thirteen percent. Why settle for thirteen lousy percent of the land?"

"This government is all powerful," Peter said. "Look how they just crush anybody who raises their head like an ant."

"People will continue to struggle until we get free," Pitso said.

"It's all foolish, fighting a losing battle," Peter said. "They're just stupid, just making themselves canon fodder. They will rot in prison without achieving anything."

Pitso walked to Peter's side of the table and waved his finger in his face. "Don't you bloody talk like that when my kid brother is being railroaded to prison by these fools," Pitso shouted. "It's cowards like you who pee in your pants when you see a white man…that's who complicates our struggle."

Peter looked around like something might leap out of the walls and bite him. "I didn't mean Tiro-"

Pitso snapped. "You control your loose tongue."

"Come on, men," Edward said, "keep this a civil discussion."

Pitso stomped outside. "Got to get out of here before I do something I'll regret."

Kagiso, who had been softly mashing squash, left the wooden spoon in the pot and followed his brother outside.

Peter put the pear on the table.

Edward took a deep labored breath. "*Motlogolo*, my sister's child, you tend to be loose with your tongue. That's one of your weaknesses. Be careful at times like these. You are lucky they are your cousins. I don't know what Pitso would've done to you if you were not. Be careful. Your young cousin is in trouble. This is no time to fool around."

"I'm sorry uncle." Peter said and hung his head.

It was hard for Edward not to feel sorry for Peter, even when he really deserved to be kicked out. Even Edward would've thrown him out, if he weren't his sister's fatherless son. Edward took his responsibility as uncle seriously, but Peter did not make it easy sometimes. The only consolation was that Peter never meant harm. He was just insensitive. People mistook this for cruelty. It was hard to tell the difference though.

"You should be glad your aunt didn't hear all this," Edward said. "There's a lot of pain here. She would've kicked you out. I'm sure. Tiro's situation is very serious. These are the things that could cause serious discord in our family. My sister has struggled hard to raise you into a decent person. Remember you're all she's got."

"I understand, uncle," Peter said. "I have to run now. Get ready for church."

Peter grabbed the unfinished pear and took a bunch of grapes from the fruit bowl. A few fell and he did not pick them up.

"I'll go open the gate for you," Edward said. "Go ahead."

Edward held the gate as Noga reversed out.

"He's leaving?" Evelyn said, still at work in the front garden.

"He says he's got some stuff to do at home before church," Edward said. "But look he's going the opposite direction. When is my sister's child going to grow up?"

Peter took off in second gear, tires screeching, and dust flying all over.

Children shouted, "Flying squad."

"Mind the children in the street!" Evelyn shouted to Peter, even though she knew he didn't hear her.

Edward sighed deeply. "This wild streak in him."

"Show off, like a child." Evelyn said. "He's so selfish you'd think on a Sunday morning he'd at least help his wife with the little ones. He could be going around with them in the car, while he's doing his up and downs. This new car is making him crazy. He's like a child with a new toy."

Edward shook his head. "Look how we all thought marriage and children would change him."

"Ah, what can we say," Evelyn said. "It's true when they say every family has all types. He's harmless but so irritating at times."

Edward thought of calling in Pitso and talking about Peter but decided to let it go. He went to sit outside on the kitchen stoop and polished his formal black shoes. Neo brought her shoes too. Edward looked at Neo and felt grateful. He missed Dikekeledi who died in the drowning accident. Neo was such a happy child, such a joy, a comfort.

Kagiso carried the trash bag to the metal can behind the garage.

This time was precious to Edward when all his children were around. Tiro's absence made the presence of the other children more intense. He wished Tiro were here. He missed him. There was a big hole in his heart, and there seemed to be all kinds of empty spaces in the house—spaces Tiro would have filled. All those empty spaces seemed to duplicate themselves inside his body.

Evelyn left for church early to attend a women's meeting. Edward and Neo walked to church together.

At the taxi terminal, they crossed the street into Section R. A young taxi driver with a khaki overcoat shouted, "S and S here, Station here!"

Another said, "Via Church Street here, via Villeria here!"

Another boasted, "Ten minutes to town."

A young boy carried a large box of Golden Delicious apples, suspended on a thick strap from his neck. He pushed the box towards them. "Three cents, one, two for six cents. Delicious apples."

Another boy shoved his small box of roasted peanuts at them "Peanuts, peanuts, best in the world."

Three women dressed in the green and yellow uniform of the Zion Christian Church greeted them, "A e ate! They said in Setswana, meaning, may peace increase."

Neo started to cross the street and Edward pulled her back. "Neo, careful."

"Ntate," Neo said. "The car is far away. It won't hit me."

"It's fast, and these taxis are always in a hurry," Edward said. "We have to be careful."

"We have to sprint," Neo said. "Otherwise it will take us forever to cross."

"Better late than never, *ngwanake*," Edward said. "They really should install a traffic light at this corner."

"Like in town," Neo said. "For white people."

There was not a single traffic light in all of Melodi.

The Methodist church in Melodi was a big, brick, two-story building. The first floor was a hall used for community activities like conferences, meetings of the women's league, Sunday School, youth club and others. Services were held on the top floor. A long stairwell from outside led directly to the main door upstairs. Teacher Molapo, with white hair and black-rimmed glasses, read the notices and announcements. There was the usual news of weddings and meetings. But the last notice, announced the death of a young man, Richard Moremi. He died from complications of torture during an interrogation by the Security police. The congregation stood and bowed their heads and the choir led in the singing of the hymn, "We remember those who have passed away."

The church was full not only because it was Youth Day but also because the minister, and not one of the lay preachers, was leading the service.

The Minister, Moruti, read the passage in the Bible about the suffering of the Jews in Egypt and preached about deliverance from oppression. As he went on with the sermon, he spoke faster and louder, to a peak, then lowered and slowed his voice until he was almost whispering. At that point the congregation became dead quiet. He paused, and then took a long audible breath.

Moruti asked all the young people under eighteen to rise. He addressed them directly and said, "on you rests tomorrow." He continued, "Since this is youth day, we'd like to recognize people who give their precious time so generously to assist with our youth. I'd like to recognize the advisor to the youth club, Teacher Noga, who over the past two years has done a lot of activities with the club. Thanks to him, the club's theater group is active and you all saw how wonderful their Christmas play was this year. And, as you all know, under Mr. Noga's direction they are hard at work on a new play about the Ten Commandments."

Some people turned around to look at Peter who smiled broadly.

Moruti continued, "Teacher Noga, please stand up so everybody can see you."

Moruti had hardly finished the sentence when Peter leapt up, squared his shoulders and adjusted his jacket. He smiled, a wide smile, turned around in all directions, and bowed. People applauded. Peter, like a child, remained standing and smiling even after the applause had died down.

"Thank you Teacher Noga," Moruti said, indicating with his arm, "you may sit down now."

Moruti asked that one of the elders pray. Oupa Kosi's deep shivering, but powerful, voice filled the church with the prayer. "We are here Father," he paused and then continued. "Father please be with the Marus at this difficult time. Their son is facing the trial of his life, Father. But you are great Lord, greater than those who have made themselves the Lords of this world." Then Oupa Kosi prayed for everybody including those in prisons and hospitals.

Edward was roused out of his thoughts by the sound of "Amen" at the end of Grandfather Koli's prayer. As soon as he started to open his eyes, another voice started praying in English. "God we bow before you..." It was Noga. He'd never prayed in church before. Well, he's getting along, growing, and he was on his knees! But Edward wished Peter wasn't praying in English, but in a language the members understood. White people in their churches wouldn't pray in anything but English or Afrikaans.

Peter continued. "We place your children before you, Father, all of them. You, whose Son said, 'Let the children come before me.' Help the older ones especially, Father, in these trying and difficult times. We pray especially for those in prison, Father. Be with them, and put light in their dark cells. Keep the children out of trouble and keep them from bad company."

Edward was relieved when Peter said, "Amen".

When Peter finally sat down, the choir sang, "On the banks of the rivers of Babylon, we sat and cried as we remembered Zion." Two men passed the collection plate around. When they were done, Moruti asked for a special collection to help the Youth Club since this was Youth Day. Two boys came to the front and held the collection dishes. A woman at the back started the hymn, "You are a merciful God." Peter was the first to get up and go to put money in the dish. He touched one of the boys on the shoulder, greeting him. A few other people followed Peter's lead.

"If you can't come to the front," Peter said. "Just raise your hand and one of these illustrious young men will be happy to come to you. And we hope, God's congregation, that you will dig deep into your pockets. These are our youth, our tomorrow."

Several women stepped to the rhythm of the hymn as they walked to the front. Many others followed.

When the last person had sat down, Moruti thanked the congregation and went back into the pulpit. "We will ask the choir to lead us in the singing of hymn number thirteen, 'Sedi la ka mponesetse tsela'…Lead kindly light."

Moruti thanked the congregation and said the closing prayer.

Outside the church, many people came to the Marus to offer their sympathies. Some women had tears in their eyes.

At home,in the kitchen, Pitso, Kagiso and their friend George played cards after dinner.

Edward and Evelyn relaxed in the living-room.

"They are not going anywhere today?" Edward asked, referring to Pitso and Kagiso.

"They are quiet these days." Evelyn said.

"This is hard on them." Edward said. "I wish there was something I could do to make it easier for them."

"Neo has already left for Koko's house." Evelyn said.

"We are lucky to have Koko," Edward said. "Neo is lucky."

Edward took a nap. He was exhausted. He needed to regain energy, tomorow was another court day. He was breaking into pieces inside but he had to look rested and strong for his son, Tiro. God knows what other lies the police were busy concocting about his child.

Evelyn rested for an hour and then went to work in the garden. She took out the dead tomato plants. Except for the cabbage plant, her vegetable garden was dead. She looked forward to spring when her garden would come to life again.

CHAPTER 11

Court-Day Two

The prosecution brought out more witnesses who repeated what the previous witnesses said.

The defense noted again that the witnesses were repeating the same unproved allegations.

The witness, Paul Musi, was on the stand now. He seemed to be swallowed by his oversized black jacket. He rubbed his red eyes.

"Mr. Musi, tell the court what Mr. Maru told you," the prosecutor said.

"He said he was going to lead an uprising against Whites and liberate black people. He was going to first direct the effort at school, and then move on to join the group in the White town and launch further attacks."

"How were they going to accomplish that?"

"He said they had amassed weapons, which they hid, and they were going to get petrol for burning the houses of white teachers and people."

"How did he describe white people?"

"He said they were all thieves, devils and dogs," Mr. Musi said. "And they should all be killed."

"No further questions, your honor." The prosecutor walked smartly back to his chair.

Mr. Brecht buttoned his navy jacket as he rose to cross-examine.

"Mr. Musi," Mr. Brecht began. "Were there any witnesses to these alleged conversations?"

"No," he said. "He only told me when we were alone, and he swore me to secrecy."

"Did he seem serious to you?" Mr. Brecht asked. "Maybe like all young men his age, the accused was just talking big to impress his friends."

"Objection, your honor. Calls for a conclusion," the prosecutor said.

"Sustained."

"Did you see the so-called weapons?" Mr. Brecht asked. "The sticks and things?"

"No"

Mr. Brecht smiled and the audience chuckled.

Mr. Brecht had no further questions.

Evelyn wondered how many more witnesses they were going to call. They were all saying the same thing. The prosecution had such a weak case. Not that it mattered—the defendant was black. They didn't need a strong case. The whole thing was a charade. Her thoughts were interrupted by the prosecutor's voice.

"The state calls to the stand Miss X," the prosecutor said.

People hissed and gasped. Hitherto, the prosecutor had not protected any witnesses.

Evelyn could not believe her eyes when Miss X came out. She blinked hard, sat up and leaned forward. "Marie! Oh my God" Evelyn took Edward's hand and squeezed. She felt anger constrict her chest. She felt like getting up and shouting, but she controlled herself.

There was mumbling in the court. "Marie" was all Evelyn heard as people whispered to each other.

Evelyn turned to Edward. "Can you believe it?"

Marie walked tall and upright. She was fair like her Colored grandmother, but under the lights, she seemed white. Her white satiny blouse shimmered in the bright light of the courtroom. She wore the blouse loose over her straight black skirt.

She shifted around, as though trying to find a perfect position, then settled and sat upright, as though she was freeing herself from the grip of her clothes. She squared her shoulders and kept her hands relaxed on her lap. Her black angora beret was tight around her head. Her long wavy hair was pulled back and it flowed from under her beret onto her back. Marie did not show much nervousness like the other witnesses. Evelyn was surprised by Marie's self-control; as though giving evidence in court was a small thing to her.

The judge banged his gavel at all the noise. "There shall be order, otherwise I'll clear the court." Even with this threat there was still hissing and whispering. The judge had to bang the gavel several times before order was restored.

The prosecutor stood about a foot from the stand and spoke slowly and gently.

"Miss X, how did you get to know about the plan?" the prosecutor asked in Afrikaans.

People mumbled. Afrikaans was the hated language of the government. All the proceedings thus far had been in English. Marie was the only one to testify in Afrikaans, and that cemented her status as a 'sellout.'

Marie held her head upright. "I heard about it on numerous occasions from one of the defendants."

"Who?"

"Tiro Maru."

"How long have you known him?"

"Since we were little," she said. "Before we started school."

"Do you recognize this letter?" the prosecutor said.

"Yes."

"Who is it addressed to?"

"Me," she said.

"Who is it from?"

"Tiro Maru," she said.

"Will you read it, please?" he said solicitously.

She held the letter with both hands and gently brought it closer to her eyes. Then, she moved it further away, then near again, finally settling on a spot. She started to read the letter aloud, slowly. "Dear Marie, all the preparations are in place now. This is my last correspondence before we spring into action and solve this problem once and for all. We shall not fail. History is on our side. We will succeed. The bark of the imperialists is worse than their bite," she paused and hung her head.

The whole thing seemed rehearsed, down to the batting of her eyelids.

The judge frowned, forming creases on his forehead. This was the first time he had shown any emotion or involvement since the trial started. He didn't seem pleased.

Evelyn sighed, and the lines on the outside edges of her eyes tightened.

The prosecutor nodded slightly. "Go on please."

"Be sure, we're not going to take the land from Dr. Vuilgoed and Company in a civil way," she read the part referring to Dr. Verwoerd, the Afrikaner Prime Minister as 'Vuilgoed' which in Afrikaans means dirt. She continued, "Wish us luck."

The judge leaned forward.

Evelyn could feel it in her bones—things were taking a sharp turn for the worse.

The defense lawyer, Mr. Brecht, stood just two feet from his table.

Evelyn knew Marie was the most credible witness so far. Even though she lived in Melodi it was obvious she had mixed heritage. It was easy for those who did not know her family to assume that one of her parents, rather than her grandmother, was Colored—of mixed black and white heritage. In the social hierarchy in South Africa, whites were at the top, coloreds in the middle, and Africans at the bottom. Marie was going to elicit the most sympathetic hearing from the white judge and his assessors. Evelyn hoped Mr. Brecht would be careful.

"Miss X, don't you think that Tiro's letter was nothing more than an impressionable seventeen-year-old young man's clumsy attempt to impress an attractive young woman such as yourself, trying to boast about being a hero, a freedom fighter?"

The prosecutor jumped up. "Objection, your honor. Calls for speculation."

Before the judge could rule, Mr. Brecht said, "No further questions, your honor."

It was drizzling when they left the court.

On the way home, they drove in silence. The rain began to fall harder, and Edward switched the windshield wipers to a faster speed.

Evelyn listened to the rhythm of the wipers. They helped soothe her racing mind.

As they drove towards Melodi, the rain seemed to fall even harder. Edward set the wipers to the third level, the fastest. There was a quick flash in the sky ahead.

"So much rain, Ntate," Neo said. "If it doesn't stop, water will drown the earth, and the ocean and the earth will be one. We will be like Noah in the ark."

"The earth is deep and it can absorb all the rain water," Edward said. He always knew how to calm Neo.

"I can't believe how ridiculous the police are," Evelyn said. "To charge Tiro with High Treason, Sabotage, and all these serious charges and then to produce no hard evidence beyond little sticks. Everybody's laughing at them. No judge with any semblance of integrity, not even an Afrikaner 'Hanging Judge', would convict on such pitiful evidence."

"You never know with these people," Edward said. "They've gone crazy and they are terrified. They see communists behind every bush. The government knows it's just an excuse but you'd be surprised how a majority of ordinary whites think people who are against Apartheid are Communists."

"Afrikaners are pathetic and ignorant. They believe anything their fascist leaders tell them," Pitso said. "And as for the English, they have only one God and that is money. Once in a while, to assuage their feeble consciences, they have to make some mild protest."

"You know what they say about English liberals," Kagiso said. "They are people with many fine principles, none of which they are prepared to die for."

Neo said, "Know the joke about the English…"

"Neo," Edward interrupted her and blew his nose.

Neo changed direction. "Afrikaners."

"Neo," This time it was Evelyn.

"Can't ever underestimate the cruelty of these monsters," Kagiso said.

"I think our struggle is entering a new phase," Pitso said.

Evelyn winked. "Careful." She did not want this conversation around Neo.

"What?" Neo said.

"High school students are becoming very politically active and joining the Movement. So, they arrest a seventeen-year-old and charge him with the highest political crimes just to make an example," Edward said.

"Nobody should use my child to prove that they are prepared to destroy all our children," Evelyn said.

"I can't believe it," Pitso said. "In the Supreme Court, they present such a weak case, and this stupid English judge sits there pretending it is all serious. I don't know why they bother having a judge. They might as well just have the police decide the sentence."

"I hope the presence of international observers and extensive publicity will help us," Edward said. "They know foreign journalists are there. I hope this puts them to shame."

"They are beyond shame," Pitso said. "Anyway, overseas people are all behind them. They are all white and in a crunch they will side with their own white people and these colonists know it. That's why they don't care."

"You can see this judge is ready to pass sentence," Pitso said. "Actually I think he wishes Tiro had committed murder so he could have the pleasure of sentencing him to death."

"You're better off with an Afrikaner judge. He doesn't have to prove he's tough and loyal to the Afrikaner cause. The English judges are tougher because they're trying to prove they are good. They want to be appointed to the Appeals court and be set for life," Evelyn said.

"There's hope," Edward said. "Let's keep praying and hoping he's acquitted."

Thunder roared. A burst of lightening flashed ahead of them.

"Ooh!" Neo was startled.

"Don't get scared my child," Edward said. "You know by the time you hear the sound, the danger is past. And, you're safe in the car because the tires absorb the electricity. This is the best place to be when there's lightning."

No one spoke, there was only the squishy sound of tires on the wet tarred street and the windshield wipers beating furiously against the windshield.

"Where's Peter today?" Kagiso asked. "It's not like him to miss anything. Definitely not an opportunity to shoot his mouth off and analyze things."

"Yes, to analyze things he knows nothing about," Pitso said. "It's probably because of yesterday's incident. He can't figure out if he should come to support Tiro. Just because he's angry with me, he doesn't come."

"What exactly did he do or say yesterday?" Evelyn said.

Edward cleared his throat.

"Nothing, really," Pitso said, "Just his usual big mouth. "He's childish," Evelyn said. "You should have seen him in church when he was recognized for his support to the Youth Club. Poor thing, it was touching. He was like a child."

Kagiso said, "How did he act, Mummy?"

Before she could answer, Edward interrupted.

"Evelyn, please don't make fun of him. He is annoying, but his work with the Youth Club is commendable. That's the good side of him. He felt proud and he deserved to. He was excited."

"That's amazing, Ntate," Pitso said. "That's something, probably the only selfless thing he's ever done in his whole life."

Kagiso said, "He always has an ulterior motive."

"Maybe he's looking for some senior position in the church and this is his way," Evelyn said.

"You people," Edward said. "My poor sister's child. I've tried to talk to him about his tendency to show off."

Evelyn shook her head. "But what can we do? And to think your sister is so sweet. How did she come to have such a fool for a son?"

"Evelyn," Edward said. "Please…"

"Sorry," Evelyn said. "You're right."

"You know, as they say," Edward said. "*e e masi ga e itsale,* A good cow that produces a lot of milk, doesn't breed similar cows."

"He made me so furious yesterday," Pitso said. "I came close to killing him. If Ntate had not been there…mm…"

Evelyn said, "You people never told me what the spat was about."

Edward cleared his throat. Fortunately his sons understood his signal. They remained silent. Thank God. It was better this way. Evelyn would have been very angry.

"It was nothing," Kagiso finally said. "You know how Noga is."

"Neo, where's my daughter?" Edward asked, changing the subject.

"Here."

"You're so quiet today," Edward said.

Evelyn smiled and turned her head to look at the back of the car where Neo sat sandwiched between her brothers.

"She's tired today," Evelyn said.

A lightning jolt seared her heart; the smile she put on for Neo melted off her face. She turned around facing front. As they passed Kilnerton, the jolt became a whirlwind inside her. Damn this white government! If they hadn't forced the beloved Kilnerton High School to close, her son wouldn't be in this mess.

Why anybody would fault their children for hating whites was beyond her. She knew that everyone in the car was feeling the same pain as they passed the red brick buildings of Kilnerton. She was glad everyone was swallowed in their own silence. She prayed the rain would stop for a while. The earth was one big river and she was determined to keep her children afloat.

CHAPTER 12

Boriki

Neo was glad the court adjourned early that day and the rain had stopped. She'd at last get a chance to play with her friends, something she missed while being away at school.

She changed clothes quickly, and went into the street. Several girls played boriki, a form of hopscotch. Neo was a bit out of practice so she had to concentrate hard. She started in the first square, and kicked the round flat tin, an old floor polish tin filled with soil to give it some weight. She hopped into the second square, her left foot, aimed against the tin. She kicked and hopped into the third square, and hobbled a bit, then she regained her balance. She bit her lower lip and prepared to kick into the next square.

She heard one of the girls shout, "Watch-out!" and she stretched her hands trying to maintain balance while looking around.

A young man with an unbuttoned red shirt that flailed around, ran past and Neo lost her balance even though the man had not touched her. She got up quickly and she was nearly hit by another running man, a municipal policeman. Then, another policeman ran past.

The first man flew over the fence without touching it.

A group of kids shouted, "Run, run." Dogs barked.

Neo and her friends ran around the corner to continue watching the chase. Boys leapt over fences behind the running men. "Black Jacks! Black Jacks! Black Jacks!" the kids shouted, the derogatory name for municipal police whose main job was to enforce the pass laws.

Neo shouted, "That's Piet 'Springbok'."

A few minutes later, the police caught the man and hand-cuffed him to another man who was joined to three more so they formed a human chain.

A woman came out of her house and shouted at the police, "Why don't you go catch real criminals instead of harassing innocent people!"

"None of your business, woman," one policeman said.

A second policeman added, "Your husband should slap your mouth shut woman!"

"My husband is not a beast like you," the woman said. "He is working, an honest real job not running around the whole day chasing innocent people."

"Black Jack, Black Jack…," the children chanted.

Neo and her friends followed the police as they marched the men towards the police station. At the corner, next to the

Baptist church with its overgrown grass in the yard, they joined the linked men to two other men cuffed together, forming a human train.

Neo pointed to one of the handcuffed men, a younger man who was barefoot, which usually meant he was picked up close to his home and not given the chance to get his shoes.

"That's Lily's brother from the other street. The one with the yellow BVD shirt, and shaved head."

One of Neo's friends, Joshua said, "He just came out of prison, that's why his head is shaved. He lives in section S."

"Run to his house," Neo said. "Maybe his family will bring his pass to the police station."

The two boys jogged in the direction of Section S.

The faces of the handcuffed men looked glum, devoid of hope. They stood with drooping shoulders and lowered heads, like cattle staring down the line at the slaughterhouse.

The policemen walked with their chests stuck out. They were proud hunters, showing off their catch at the end of a successful day.

The short policeman with three green stripes on his khaki shirt, waddled with his arms held away from his body.

One of the handcuffed men shouted, "I just forgot my pass! It's at home! Just two streets down."

The short policeman with his potbelly slung over his belt said, "Shut up! The law says you must have it on you at all times. Don't you know the law? Eh! Eh!"

"My pass is okay. My boss just forgot to sign it this month. Look at it," said a man in blue overalls, with the name "Ellerines" on the front pocket.

He might as well have been talking to a pole. No one responded.

"These policemen, most of them can't read!" Neo said to the kids around her. They laughed.

A crowd gathered, and watched as the police on bikes led the men towards the police station.

A woman balancing a big can of sorghum beer on her head, spit on the ground loudly. "They are dogs."

"They are afraid of the real *tsotsis,*" said a mother with an infant on her back.

Neo and her friends went back to their street and sat on the lawn of Noli's house. Neo had seen many arrested before but it had never touched her so deeply. Her friends finally stood up and started playing, but when it was her turn, she wouldn't play.

"Why?" Sall asked.

"Too tired," Neo said.

As she thought about those handcuffed men, Neo saw the face of her brother, Tiro, and felt sad.

A boy from another street ran into the Marus' yard. Neo ran over to see what he wanted.

"There's no one home," She said. "Just me."

The boy could hardly talk, he was out of breath. "Your brother," he panted. "Police."

"Which brother? Where?" Neo said, impatiently, "Tell me, tell me!"

"The Black Jacks are leading him to the police station, saw them at Section F," the boy said, still gasping for breath

"Which brother?" Neo pleaded. "Tall, short?"

"The tall one," the boy said. "Kagiso"

Neo ran into her brothers' bedroom. She found one pass on the dressing-table. It was Kagiso's as she had hoped. She knew the drill.

She jogged to the police station and as she neared, she saw the chain of handcuffed men moving towards her. Her brother, Kagiso, was one of them. She tried to hand him his pass but his handcuffs prevented it.

Kagiso raised his right hip. "Here, put it in this pocket."

Neo did as he said.

A policeman pulled at her. "Get away from here!" The policeman took the pass and scrutinized it. "Oh, Maru, you are Mistress's child at the corner there."

Kagiso didn't reply; just bit his lower lip, and looked at him.

Neo spoke up. "Yes, and he goes to school.".

"Your mother taught my child," the man said. "Good Mistress." He ordered a younger policeman to unshackle Kagiso.

Neo and Kagiso walked towards home together.

"I ran real fast," Neo said.

Kagiso took her hand. "You are the best sister in the world! Good you ran very fast before they could register us inside the police station. We would've had to wait until tomorrow to appear before the magistrate and pay fines. I would've spent the night in there."

Neo looked back at the red brick building with the rolled barbed wire fence and was glad her brother was coming home with her. She couldn't bear to think of him staying in that scary building.

Neo smiled with pride. She had helped Kagiso, but she felt a jolt of lightning and thunder inside as she remembered Tiro. She didn't say anything...just kept walking quickly away from the police.

CHAPTER 13

Trial

Evelyn was exhausted by the trial. It seemed like an endless nightmare with an endless line of witnesses. She could understand the betrayals by Tiro's friends. They weren't family friends, and they were only trying to save their skin. But Marie? The many times Evelyn had helped her mother. They had been through so much. If it hadn't for Evelyn, Marie's father would still be beating them all. What made it worse was that Marie got on the stand so coolly, as though nothing was at stake. But there was a lot at stake. Her child's freedom! Today again, they had to listen to the repetition of the same boring story from witnesses about those little weapons. It would have all been silly and funny if the outcome didn't affect her son's freedom.

After the first recess, when the court marshal said, "All rise," she felt like not standing. But then, remembered they had her child and some silly Boer policeman might take it out on Tiro later in the cells.

The judge and his two assessors took their seats.

Mr. Snyman got up, squared his shoulders, and adjusted his tie. He seemed more cocky today, Evelyn thought. It was understandable—even with a weak case like this, the odds were always on the prosecution's side. No black person expected impartiality in a political trial—not even from the judge. But for some reason, Evelyn thought the prosecutor's cockiness was based on something more. She fidgeted in her seat.

"The state calls witness number six, Mr. X."

Even though they'd been told about the mystery witness, Evelyn was shocked when Edward's nephew, Peter, walked into the box, without looking sideways.

"What?" Evelyn exclaimed. "Real snake, true to his name! Bloody fool."

The rumblings were louder today than when Marie had been in court.

"It's Noga, Mummy," Neo said, her voice full of shock.

"He has no shame," Evelyn hissed. "The dog. We fed him. Now he turns and kills our children." Evelyn turned to Edward. "Your sister's child."

"Can't believe it," Edward whispered, shaking his head slowly.

"Traitor," a man shouted in the gallery.

"*Mpimpi*. Sellout," another man shouted.

The judge pounded his gavel. "Order in my court, or I will clear the gallery!"

Evelyn squeezed Edward's moist hand. His eyes glistened as he sat silently.

"It's all right, my dear," Evelyn said. "It's not your fault. You cannot be held responsible."

The prosecutor folded his arms, and stood a few feet away from Peter, who didn't have to say his name since he was a protected witness.

"How long have you known the defendant?"

"Since he was about a month old."

"What is your relationship to the defendant?"

"He is my cousin."

There were more gasps and mumbling from the gallery.

"Please tell the court the content of your conversations with the defendant a week before his arrest."

"I went to his class on Friday afternoon during study period and called him outside." Peter said.

"Why did you disturb your cousin during study period?"

"He had asked me the day before to see him before I went home to Melodi on Friday. He wanted me to deliver something for him, and I thought he wanted me to take a letter or something to his parents."

"What happened?"

Peter said, "I was surprised when he gave me a letter to this boy I knew to be a trouble maker."

"So what did you think?"

"I was surprised and concerned," Peter said, looking straight ahead, but not seeming to focus on anything in particular.

"Why were you concerned?"

"I was shocked that Tiro would have anything to do with Khoza, who everyone knows is a trouble-maker."

"Why did you think Khoza was a trouble-maker?"

"He had caused a lot of trouble at the old school, Kilnerton. He was expelled after fomenting a strike two years ago."

"So what did you do?"

"I indicated to Tiro that I did not wish to carry anything to Khoza and I couldn't go to his home. He was not the kind of person I wished to associate with."

"Then what happened?"

"Tiro begged me, and said it was important. So I reluctantly agreed to take the letter."

"What other instructions did Tiro give you?"

"He repeated several times over, emphasizing, that I should deliver the letter personally to Khoza and no one else."

"Did you deliver the letter?"

"No."

"Why not, when your cousin begged you so much?"

"I felt uneasy about the whole thing and I postponed delivering it, hoping Tiro would forget about it and the whole thing would just go away."

"Did Mr. Tiro Maru forget about it?"

"No."

"What happened?"

"When I got to the staff room on Monday morning, Tiro was waiting for me at the door."

"How did he seem to you?"

"Objection, Your Honor. Calls for speculation," Mr. Brecht said.

"Sustained," the judge drawled.

"What happened?"

"We stepped aside, and Tiro asked me if I had delivered the letter."

"What did you tell him?"

"I told him I had."

"You lied?"

"Yes."

"Why?"

"I was trying to keep my cousin away from bad influences."

The prosecutor handed Peter a letter. "Is this the letter?"

"Yes."

"Can you read it, please?"

Peter sat up straight, and coughed. It seemed like a fake cough. He read. "Dear Comrade, regarding plans for the 22nd. All preparations have been made. I've given everybody their instructions and explained that anybody who messes up will be dealt with harshly by the organization. I made it quite clear what I meant by that. So, they are all ready to go into action." He paused, then continued. "We have assembled all the weapons, and bought the paraffin for burning the school and the teachers' cars. The timing will have to be perfect. We will kill all white teachers and any other whites around. They are not teachers, they are all a bunch of spies and propagandists who are here to teach black children to accept their oppression. I hope you are all ready. It is important that we do it together at the same time. It's a pity we cannot get guns. But we still should be able to inflict maximum damage to the enemy. Timing is important. We have to send the country up in smoke all at once, so their forces cannot cope. We will overwhelm them. So, when the boys waiting at the border come in, we can just take over. See you at the Revolution. Comrade Tiro"

"Sellout! Sellout!" a man shouted in the public gallery.

"Order!" The judge slammed his gavel.

Evelyn noticed how Tiro stared at Peter throughout, but Peter didn't look in his direction. He didn't even have the courage to glance at Tiro.

Tiro's advocate rose to cross-examine. "Mr. Noga, how long have you known Tiro's father?"

"All my life."

"What's your relationship to him?"

"My uncle. He's my mother's brother."

"Who put you through school and Teacher-Training College?"

"My uncle."

"The defendant's father?"

"Yes."

"How often do you go to Tiro's home?"

"Often."

"So, Tiro's family has been good to you. In fact, it's because of Tiro's family that you are a teacher today. Tiro's parents supported you after your own father abandoned you when you were a little boy. True?"

"Yes...true."

"Do you consider yourself trustworthy?"

"Yes."

"So why did you not deliver the letter your cousin asked you to?"

"Because Khoza is a trouble-maker, and I wanted to protect my cousin."

"Since he's your family, did you think to talk to your uncle?"

"No?"

"Some concern," Advocate Brecht said. "Did you receive any money for your work with the police?"

Peter hesitated, then said, "No."

The lawyer stepped back slowly as though it would be dangerous to turn his back to Peter. He wrinkled his nose as though there was a foul smell. "Are you a police informer, Mr. Noga?"

The prosecutor jumped. "Objection, Your Honor"

"Withdrawn." Mr. Brecht walked back to his seat.

"Mr. Brecht, be careful," the judge said, and then leaned over and whispered something to one of his two assessors.

Peter walked to a seat near the prosecutor. He looked straight ahead.

Evelyn felt like strangling Peter. She would definitely kick him out like a dog if he dared to set foot in her house ever again.

After a short break the prosecutor rose to give his closing argument. He stood in front of his table and faced the judge.

He pointed to Tiro and spoke slowly. "That is a dangerous young man." He emphasized each word.

"When you think that he is young, small and only seventeen years old, you could be fooled. His hateful actions nearly killed many. Because of the diligent courageous work of our security forces, several innocent people, including his dedicated teachers were saved."

He paused to let his words sink in.

Evelyn felt nothing but raw hate for him.

"He deliberately planned and coordinated the attack, and intimidated others into carrying out his plan. He accumulated weapons, which at first glance might not seem dangerous, but who can survive a hard blow with a pipe, even a rubber pipe? Who would survive being burned with petrol? Even though the petrol was said to have been purchased for burning cars, who really knows given the hate of the defendant? He probably would have burnt innocent people. What a cruel death for people who were there to teach him.

"This young man who has sat there calmly throughout these deliberations is dangerous, and there is no doubt that if given a chance he would still carry out his original plan.

"Society needs to be protected against such evil. He is part of the movement to overthrow the government and to kill white people. The only sentence that will stop him is the death sentence. Let's not wait until he commits murder. Your honor, the state calls for the death sentence."

There was a roar in the court.

Evelyn tried to shout, but her voice remained trapped in her tight throat. She felt dazed. Her eyes burned and she had a hard time focusing on her son who looked like a disappearing shadow. She fought hard to focus, and brought him into clear view. Her sweet son. What an evil man, this prosecutor.

Women started crying, some loudly.

There were various outbursts, "What?"

"Death for a child?"

"He did not kill anybody."

The judge pounded the gavel harder, but it took a while for the room to become silent.

Police dragged out a man in the back.

The Marus held hands. Edward had tears in his eyes. Evelyn fought to make sure her tears stayed buried deep inside.

Mr Brecht walked towards Tiro. He adjusted his black robes. Then, he began his closing argument. "The accused is a seventeen year old child. He simply allowed himself to be drawn into the movement. It is common knowledge that young men his age everywhere have notions of grandeur and of saving the world.

"The court should take this into account and weigh as important the fact that the plan did not spring from the mind of the accused. He is a young man and because of his youth he was carried away with the ideas of men much older than himself. The instigation came from men old enough to be his father. Those men have fled the country. The court should be careful not to make this young man, who has never been in trouble before, take punishment for the crimes of men the state cannot apprehend. Yes, even if all that was said was true, and that is doubtful, no one can believe that little stones, and some tubing and one gallon of petrol could be the weapons of someone who seriously intended to overthrow the state. There is no High Treason here and there is no Sabotage. The evidence is not compelling, and the defense calls for the acquittal of this young man."

Evelyn thought that surely no judge, even a white South African judge could sentence anyone to a lengthy term based on such flimsy claims. But she was still terrified. Hard to tell these days. Edward leaned over and whispered to Evelyn, "I'm worried about my child. Look at him, so young."

Neo cried softly. Edward put his arm around her. "It's going to be all right, you'll see."

Evelyn felt rumbling inside, fear exploded in her head, in her heart, in her stomach, everywhere.

The judge looked as calm and cold as he did through most of the trial. "Sentence will be passed tomorrow." He banged the gavel and said, "The court will adjourn until tomorrow morning at nine." He got up quickly and left. His assessors followed.

On the way home that day the Marus were quiet, each lost in their own thoughts. Edward blew his congested nose a lot. He felt helpless. He was in a hurry to get home and sit by the fire. It was not raining, and Edward was thankful. But, the clouds were heavy. His cold was getting worse. He could hardly breathe.

Chapter 14

News

Edward sat next to the fire, with his pipe in his mouth. It was not even lit. He was thinking about what the prosecutor had said and all the possible sentences. He played out in his mind why the judge would not impose a long sentence. Tiro was young and the case was not strong.

The prosecutor was crazy to even think of asking for the death sentence. Tiro had not hurt anybody. Even the Afrikaners could not be that crazy and cruel in full view of the whole world. Thick as they were, even they should care a little bit about the opinion of others. They had to be aware of the Amnesty International representative and others. But the Boers were crazy. The thought terrified him.

Neo sat next to him, interrupting his thoughts.

"It is almost seven," Edward said. "Neo, bring the small transistor from my bedroom."

Neo stood and came back with the radio. Evelyn, who was in the bedroom followed Neo.

Edward took a deep breath when Neo sat next to him again. He looked at his daughter then at Evelyn. "Maybe it would be better for Neo to stay at home tomorrow. Things might get a bit rough."

Neo jumped from her chair with a screech, knocking it over. She tripped, but Evelyn grabbed her by the arm.

"No, no, no, Ntate! You promised I'd attend. I didn't do anything wrong during the trial." Neo shook her head vigorously. "No, no no! I'm going, I'm going!"

"Sh, sh…" Edward tried to calm his daughter. He straightened her chair and extended his arm.

"It's all right, Neo," Edward said. "Come, sit down. No need to cry. Let's talk about it calmly."

Neo pulled away, then moved towards her father and returned to her seat. She wiped her tears with the back of her hand. "It's all unfair, it's my brother too."

"I know," Edward said. "But-"

Neo interrupted. "I must go."

Evelyn wished she and her husband had talked first. Then maybe they would've found a way to convince Neo. But knowing her, Evelyn doubted that anything would've convinced Neo. Evelyn remained silent, letting Edward handle their daughter. Neo adored her father. Evelyn did not want

Neo to be mad with her. She wanted to be able to comfort her after the sentencing.

They were all silent for a moment that seemed to last forever.

Neo folded the sleeves of her red wool sweater at the wrist. The skin on her wrist itched so she took her watch off.

Evelyn looked at the red coals through the iron grid on the open door on the front of the stove.

Edward gave Neo his handkerchief, and she sneezed. She looked at her father then her mother.

"I'm going, right?" Neo asked softly.

"I guess it will be all right, my dear," Evelyn said.

"Yes," Edward said. "But I worry about you getting hurt, Neo. Can't predict what will happen tomorrow. People are angry and the Boers are crazy."

"I'll be very, very careful, Ntate," Neo said. "If he's found guilty, is he going to be sent to Robben Island?"

"Yes," Edward said. "But let's hope for the best."

"They say the government never loses in political trials," Neo said. "The judges are all the same, eager to put blacks in prison."

There was a knock. Koko came in, wearing a heavy brown coat and woolen knitted cap.

Edward got up. "It's biting cold, Koko, come and sit here." He offered her the chair nearest the coal stove.

"It's a strange winter," Koko said. "All these clouds, all this rain, all this thunder, all this lightning. The fury of the heavens."

"This is a strange year," Edward said.

"What time are you leaving for court in the morning?" Koko said.

"You're not planning on going tomorrow, Ma?" Evelyn asked.

"No." Koko shook her head. "I'm spending the night here. I just want to make sure to get up early enough to make oats so you won't get hungry if it turns out to be a long day."

"Won't be long, Koko," Edward said. "It's just passing sentence, though sometimes some judges do take long with summation. But this one looks like the brief type."

Another knock. Kagiso and his friend George walked in.

"Mother says to tell you their prayers are with you, Mistress," George said. "She's going to be in court tomorrow."

Everybody thanked him.

"George is spending the night, Mummy." Kagiso said.

"Of course," Evelyn said, "George has stayed over many times. He knows he's always welcome." Evelyn took George's hand. "You're a child of this family too."

Koko smiled and looked at Neo. "Who's going to stay with me tomorrow?"

"No Koko," Neo said quickly. "I'm going."

Koko looked at Evelyn, who winked back.

"We should go to bed early," Evelyn said. "My dear, with your cold, you should go to bed immediately."

"Yes," Edward said. "I'll just take my medication and go to sleep. I'll listen to the late news first."

The radio announcer in a smooth calm voice said, "Four black men were shot by the police as government workers moved people from their village near Naboomspruit to their new home in Mankwe. The area, one of the most fertile, is to be used for farming. A police spokesman said police had to open fire as many black men advanced towards them and stoned government vehicles, trying to set them on fire."

"And they are surprised that people want to kill Whites?" Evelyn commented.

"Whites want to take the whole country, even the small bits occupied by people," Kagiso said.

The announcer continued. "Tomorrow, in Pretoria, sentence will be passed in the Supreme Court, in the trial of a seventeen-year-old black man, Tiro Maru, a student at Hebron High School, north of Pretoria. The trial, which has been going on since last week, has attracted record crowds including many foreign journalists and observers. Heavy attendance is expected tomorrow. A police spokesman said they expected no problems. Just in case, the police will be ready and will do everything to maintain law and order."

Edward sighed deeply. He took off his glasses and wiped his face with his handkerchief.

Later that night, Edward and Evelyn lay in bed staring at the ceiling.

Edward sneezed. "This cold is going to kill me."

"After tomorrow, you can rest and it will get better," Evelyn said. "It's made worse by the strain of the trial."

Silence.

Evelyn finally said, "I don't want my son to be punished for everybody who ran away before the police could catch them. The police are angry because a lot of the senior people in the party have fled the country."

"I worry they are going to use my child to show that they are prepared to be tough with kids," Edward said. "Even the Boers should have some shame. I don't know why I say the Boers when it's all of them, whites."

"You know what Pitso used to say, "Evelyn said. "The only difference between the Boers and the English is that the English would like the chains on Africans to be a little loose, but not so loose they can wiggle out of them."

Edward turned to sleep on his left side. "I'm getting more congested. I can't sleep with this cold. I'm going to toss and turn the whole night from one side to the other to relieve congestion. Maybe I should just go and sit on the couch in the living room, instead of disturbing you."

"No, no," Evelyn said. "You have to sleep, otherwise you'll be worse tomorrow."

Evelyn turned on the light, opened the small green can on the table and took out throat lozenges. "Have another one. It will soothe your throat."

Evelyn didn't sleep much that night. She knew Edward was not sleeping either. He coughed, sneezed and twisted the whole night.

Neo was glad Koko decided to spend this night. Neo was scared and she would've kept the light on the whole night had Koko not been there. They say creatures of the night cannot sneak in when lights are on. The problem was, Neo couldn't fall asleep with the lights on.

"Pray, Neo, we have to sleep right away tonight, so tomorrow you won't be tired," Koko said.

Neo got out of bed and knelt on the floor and rested her hands on the bed. "Which prayer would you like, Koko? The Goodnight one or the Lord's Prayer, or a special prayer?"

"Which prayer do you feel like saying? Say the one that comes first to your lips."

Neo began, "God, today my prayer is special because my brother is in the biggest trouble. Please help him, God. Don't let him go to prison where he will be tortured and beaten."

The images of prison brought hot tears that ran off her face. She cried unable to continue.

"Neo, come and kneel here on my bed next to me."

Neo turned around and did as she was told. Koko placed her hand on Neo's head as her granddaughter shook with sniffles.

"It's all right to pray even when we're crying," Koko said. "God will comfort you."

Neo started again. "God, please help my brother." She cried again. Koko gave her a handkerchief and she cleared her nose, but continued to cry.

"Neo," Koko said. "Tell you what. Let's say the Lord's Prayer together. That will help because it takes care of everything.

Let's do it together. Our Father, Who art in heaven, hallowed be thy name…"

Neo joined and they prayed slowly. A while later, Neo's tears went away.

When they were done, Neo got up. She tried to turn the bedside lamp on, but it didn't work. She went to the door and turned off the big overhead light and dashed to her bed.

They were quiet for a while.

"Koko?"

"Yes."

"Why is it all the witches don't come together and bewitch all the white people?"

"Why?"

"Because they're very bad people and the witches should bewitch them all and kill them. Oh, but maybe killing is a sin. So the witches should bewitch all the white people and not kill them, but make them into *tokoloshes* and make them work hard at night." Neo said this in a rushed breath so she was gasping at the end.

Koko said, "Remember how we agreed we don't want to be like white people because we don't want our souls to be soiled by hate?"

"I don't want to be like them," Neo said. "Maybe the witches should make them just go back where they came from, to Europe."

"God is with us," Koko said. "All this will come to an end."

"Goodnight," Koko said. "Your grandfather and all your ancestors are watching over you. So don't be afraid. Just close your eyes and sleep."

"Goodnight, Koko."

After a long silence, there was the sound of something dully falling in the side street, and a dog barked.

"What's that?" Neo said, pulling up her covers to her chin.

"Just dogs playing outside and barking at other dogs."

Thank God Koko is here, Neo thought. Finally, she fell asleep.

But Neo was soon awake again. "Koko I can't sleep."

"Let's sing 'ke lapile ke a lala, matlho a ka a fifala. Ntate yo Legodimong, O mpoloke bosigong'" Koko sang in her soothing voice. "I'm tired, I'm sleeping, My eyes are darkening, Father in Heaven, watch over me tonight."

It was a goodnight song that Koko taught Neo when she was a small child. Neo liked it. They sang it over and over until Neo yawned and stopped singing. Koko sang it one more time after Neo stopped. They finally fell asleep.

Chapter 15

Sentencing

It was still dark outside when Evelyn got up on the day of sentencing. She turned on the electric heater in their bedroom and went to the kitchen. She started the coal stove.

Then she made tea, put two filled cups on a tray along with Edward's medicine and went back to her bedroom.

Edward lay on his side and swallowed two pills with water. Evelyn sat on the dressing-table chair and faced him. Both drank their tea quietly for a while.

"It's still early, "Evelyn said. "You can lie down for a while." She waited until Edward fell asleep, then she returned to the kitchen.

Evelyn opened the kitchen door and stood on the stoop. Even though the sun had not risen yet, a few people were already going to work. Night was departing, while day light was struggling to break through. It was not clear yet whether the sky would be overcast or whether it was just the shadow of the night still hanging.

She stood there for a long while and drank a second cup of tea. The weak morning light edged out the dark shadows. A thin sharp wind blew through the bare trees which were stripped of leaves and life. The trees looked like collections of dry dead twigs. One would swear they'd never come to life again.

She heard the milkman's bell, which sounded thin and sharp and grated on her ears like tin being filed. The sun finally came out, but it didn't have much luster around it.

Evelyn returned to the kitchen, stoked the stove and added more coal. She wanted the kitchen to be warm when everybody got up.

The Marus got to court an hour early, but the crowd that was already there was larger than it was on any of the days before. People offered encouragement.

A young man they had not seen before said, "All the sell-outs will pay for what they are doing to our people. We will deal with them, Mistress." Evelyn thought he could be one of her former students.

A few photographers took pictures.

The minister of their church greeted them. "Thank you for coming, Reverend," Edward said.

The police were everywhere, with vans parked next to the court. They closed the block to traffic.

"Look Mummy," Neo said as she pointed to army tanks parked on both ends of the street. "Hippos and soldiers over there."

Police with dogs paraded among the crowd.

The Marus walked to the front doors of the court and when they opened, they were the first in. They sat in the second row, the same row they had occupied throughout the trial.

The judge stroked his hair back, adjusted his shiny gold-rimmed glasses and summarized the trial.

"The state," he began, "has proved beyond all doubt that the defendant planned sabotage and planned to be part of the effort to overthrow the state. The defendant planned to murder his white teachers, people who were dedicated to his upliftment. The defendant is a dangerous young anarchist. Had it not been for his age, I would have imposed the death sentence."

There was a huge collective gasp and murmurs from the gallery.

Evelyn could not believe it. "My God" she whispered.

Neo shouted, "No!" She cried.

Edward put his arm around Neo.

"*Amandla a wethu!*" Some shouted. "Power is ours!"

The judge called for order. When the courtroom was finally silent, he continued. "Given the defendant's age, I sentence him to life in prison."

Tiro jumped up and raised his hands and shouted, "Amandla! Amandla!."

Tiro looked at his parents as he was being led away by the guards.

"My son, my son," Edward said.

"Amandla! Amandla! Amandla!" came from the gallery.

Evelyn's head felt hollow and inside a tornado swirled against its walls. Her stomach cramped. It was as if her head and body threatened to separate as she struggled to keep them together. Her head was about to explode. She touched her temples for an instant and that seemed to quiet the storm somewhat. She couldn't believe this white judge was talking about her seventeen-year-old son.

"My son in prison for life?" Evelyn said, "These Boers have gone crazy now. They'll pay. They are not God. Monsters!"

Neo sobbed and her whole body shook. "I don't want Tiro to go to prison. My brother." She buried her head in Evelyn's chest.

Evelyn held her.

Edward rubbed Neo's head.

As they tried to leave, people crowded them, trying to console them. The police were all over, commanding everybody to leave the building. The Marus walked down the steps to the curb.

Photographers took their pictures. Light bulbs popped. A white reporter asked, "Mr. Maru, how do you feel about this?"

A big dark cloud hung ominously above, as though it would break and the water would fall at once, and crush everyone below.

A man shouted at a journalist, "Leave them alone!"

Some young men surrounded the Marus and tried to help them make their way out. Evelyn had her arm around Neo, who was still crying. Tears streamed freely down her cheeks.

One of the white reporters pleaded and stuck his microphone out. "Mr. Maru, one comment please. Sir, how do you feel?"

Edward stopped. "Devastated." He spoke slowly, his hoarse voice barely audible. Then he looked down and wiped the sweat off his forehead. Finally, he lifted his head and strained to raise his cracking voice. "This is the saddest day for my family, the saddest day of my life. I wish I could take my son's place."

"There will be justice one day," Evelyn said and was about to go on, when she remembered they had her son. She didn't want the police taking anything out on him.

The crowd sang the struggle song in Zulu. "This burden is mine, and I will carry it to the end. This land is mine, and I will take it back."

Evelyn leaned towards Edward's ear. "Should we leave now? Your fever seems to be getting worse."

"Let's wait a bit," Edward said. "Maybe they'll do it the usual way and Tiro can see us as his van passes. He'll feel strengthened."

People lined both sides of the street. The van with bullet-proof windows and bars came from the back and as soon as it appeared, people sang louder and stomped on the ground harder.

Some women cried. Some boys chanted, "Kill the Boers. Kill the dogs. Kill the whites. One white, one bullet."

Police with dogs kept people out of the street. Some girls in school uniforms managed to break through. They ran into the street in the path of the van. It stopped. Police had their guns drawn ready to shoot.

One of the dogs caught a girl's leg and she screamed. People screamed. The police dragged the girl out of the street.

The van continued on its way and speeded up. People continued to sing and shout cries of "Amandla!"

Evelyn, Edward and Neo stood huddled together against the cold wind and watched the van speed away. They waved.

A woman changed the song and the crowd sang, "*Kaofela Morena o re thuse re bone Matlhogonolo. Jwale ke tsatsi la ho qetela, kaofela Morena o re thuse, re bone Matlhogonolo.* God help us all to see blessings. This is the last day. God help us see blessings."

Evelyn felt as though her heart had swollen to fill her whole chest and it was about to explode. She hugged Neo and took Edward's arm.

"I'm right here," Kagiso said, and George was with him.

"My children, you two should be careful." Edward said.

Evelyn was relieved when they got into the car and drove home.

Neo continued to cry.

"This may be our darkest hour," Evelyn said. "But they've not won as long as we pick up the pieces and continue."

"It's all going to come to an end one day, Auntie," George said.

"They are crazy now," Evelyn said. "They are prepared to jail you even if you sneeze the wrong way."

"Is he going to stay in prison all his life?" Neo asked, haltingly.

"No," Evelyn said. "We are going to be free."

They drove home, quiet most of the way.

Koko leaned against the brick wall of the house and waited. It seemed as if she'd been there forever.

Kagiso opened the gate and the wooden garage doors. Edward pulled the car into the garage. They got out.

Edward dragged himself out of the car, opened the door half-way to avoid hitting the piles of boxes that leaned precariously against the wall. He slid from the car sideways and cringed when he bumped his head against the car roof. He lifted his head and stroked it, beginning with the bald shiny spot in front, working towards the thick fold at the back of his head, and down his neck. He looked up, took off his glasses and rubbed his nose between the eyes.

Neo closed the garage door. "Thank you, my child," he said.

He closed the left door of the garage while Neo closed the right. He trudged towards the house's back door. His shoulders were round and he looked like a body without a neck.

Neo tiptoed behind him as if to avoid upsetting the trembling earth. She wiped her hands on her dress. The thought of a death sentence for her brother sent a chill rippling through her body.

"No, it cannot be," Neo mumbled to herself. "God, please don't let it be."

Her father lifted one leg then the other to climb the four steps at the stoop. He went into the kitchen. Edward paused for a moment and sighed, as though he had just finished climbing a high mountain. He was wondering how he was going to make it back down. He held his gray jacket with both hands.

He sighed deeply as though afraid there would be no air left for the next round.

"We heard it on the radio. Life for what? He didn't kill anybody," Koko said. "Oh my child's child."

"They say he was the leader," Edward said.

The earth spun and the light got dimmer. Neo's eyes burned. She looked down at the floor to steady her head but the alternating black and white floor tiles made her more dizzy. She looked up at the ceiling, but it also spun around. She held on to the chair tightly. Her mother's hand on the back of her head steadied her and Neo took a deep breath.

Her brother in prison for the rest of his life. Her brother would be in prison even when he became an old man.

Evelyn asked, "How can this be when he is only eighteen, just a child."

"I'm sorry," Edward apologized, as though it were his fault.

He shuffled towards the opposite end of the table, pulled a chair and sat down. He removed his glasses and placed them gently on the table. He rubbed the sides of his nose where the glasses made ridges. He wiped his eyes.

He leaned on the table, his hand supporting his jaw and his elbow anchored by the table. He lifted his head and declared, without a lot of energy, more to himself than to anybody else, "Proud of him. He's a brave man, my son."

Neo brought a glass of water to Edward and he took a few small sips. He put the glass on top of the embroidered red rose on the white tablecloth and coughed.

"Bring his medication," Evelyn said.

"This flu is going to kill me," Edward said.

"Go to bed, my dear," Evelyn said.

"No, I'm fine." He took the bottle from Neo and drank the dark brown syrup. He put the bottle down gently and took out his white handkerchief and wiped his glistening face.

"Go to bed, my dear. Everybody will understand," Evelyn said. "Eat some soup and go to bed."

"I'll lie down a little bit." He stood to go to the bedroom.

"Before you sleep Ntate, would you like a cup of tea?" Neo asked. "I'll make sure to warm the milk."

"Yes, my child." Edward walked slowly into his room.

In the kitchen Neo leaned against the sink and looked through the window into the backyard. The vine climbing over the garage was bare. It was hard to imagine that in the spring it would come to life again. To the right, the peach tree looked like a collection of dead twigs, precariously held together but unconnected. The garden, where during the Christmas season plump juicy tomatoes, crisp lettuce, dark green spinach and string beans thrived, looked barren.

She coughed to clear the lump in her throat. She gripped the shiny faucet. The earth beneath her began to spin again.

She went outside to breathe. The air was crisp. A passing car whipped a thick cloud of dust that blew in all directions. She saw Pitso, Kagiso and their friend George, who stood talking at the gate. She wondered if they too would be sent to prison. She felt short of breath.

The only people she knew who were in prison were Zorro and Chicks—they waylaid people, robbing them at night. They were tsotsis—nothing but thugs.

Neo thought of the prisoners she saw working at the zoo, and she tried to imagine Tiro in a khaki prison uniform. But Robben Island where Tiro was going was so far. He was going to be surrounded by water. The thought terrified her. It was a nightmare. Would they beat them everyday on the island?

She went back into the kitchen, and stoked the fire, adding more wood and coal in the stove. She looked at the sparks from the burning wood and they seemed to be jumping about like wild, wiry, dancing skeletons. She thought about her father's cold and how weak he looked. What if he died? What would happen to them? She looked at the window and counted eight panels. She contemplated the expanse of blue on the wall. It seemed deep and endless like the sky. She imagined big white policemen with scary faces pummeling her brother Tiro with clubs and sjamboks. Hot tears filled her eyes but she suppressed them; they stayed suspended and weighed her head down.

There was a knock on the door and Mr. Mota, a member of their church, walked into the house. He took off his black felt hat and held it in his hands. He hugged Neo.

"Neo, how are you my child?"

"Fine," Neo said softly.

"It's going to be all right," Mr. Mota said.

"Joe, glad to see you," Koko said. "Come in, Evelyn is in the living room."

"I'm sorry," Mr. Mota said.

"Thank you Joe," Koko said.

In the living room Evelyn offered Mr. Mota a seat.

"Sad news," Mr. Mota said, "I'm very sorry."

"Well, that's the news," Evelyn said. "What can we say?"

"A seventeen year old who hasn't killed anybody?" Mr. Mota said. "No guns, no weapons, little sticks and things."

"Let's just hope this is an aberration," Evelyn said. "Not a new pattern where they're going to hang our children for any little thing. We just thank God it's not a death sentence."

"Life," Mr. Mota said. "After that sham trial, he came in ready to give out a life sentence. You could just see it, that devil, an English judge for that matter. We expect the Afrikaner judges to be hangmen, but it's just like the English. Their mask of civility hides an unfathomable deadliness. All whites are just the same."

"But you know what they always say," Evelyn said. "The English judges are worse because they have to prove they are tough. The English have always been snakes."

"It's all going to end some day," Mr. Mota said.

"They can't do this to our children and get away with it," Evelyn said. "They'll pay."

Edward came out of the bedroom and joined Evelyn and Mr Mota in the living room. "I thought I heard your voice, Joe."

Mr. Mota got up and the two men shook hands. "

"I'm sorry about Tiro," Mr. Mota said. "I can't believe it." He shook his head.

They sat on the couch.

"They're sending all the political prisoners to Robben Island-" Edward did not finish the sentence. He coughed and rested his head back against the couch.

"That's a bad cold," Mr. Mota said.

"You're right, Joe," Evelyn said. "It's this strange winter with rain."

Evelyn took Edward's arm. "Come on, dear"

Joe got up and hovered, trying to help.

"Joe," Edward said. "Thank you for coming. Sorry I can't stay. This medication makes me drowsy."

Edward went back to bed.

Evelyn and Joe continued to talk about the trial.

That afternoon and into the night they were joined by various relatives, friends and neighbors. It was like a wake. Visitors included members of the Women's Union from their church, teachers from Evelyn's school.

They talked about Peter. "That snake. He will never set his dirty feet in my house again," Evelyn said. "I don't even want to think what I'd do to him. Sell my child, then come into my house? That will be the day. Let him just try it. I'll chase him out like a dog."

"Don't worry," one of the women said. "He'll get his punishment one day."

"The money he made selling my child's blood will not do him any good," Evelyn said. "It will evaporate into thin air."

"Peter has always been a dog," Mr. Mota said. "He prances about in his new bloody car like he owns the world. It's dripping with our children's blood. Now we know where he got the money to build a rich man's house."

In the kitchen Koko made tea and Neo arranged cups and saucers on two trays.

Goerge's mother Ma-Malamba joined them. She hugged Neo. "Don't worry, my child. Your brother will get out of prison."

Neo didn't say anything.

Ma-Malamba dabbed tears with her handkerchief and then hugged Koko. "God is there, Koko."

"We should never doubt that," Koko replied. "No matter how bleak things look. If we lose our faith, then the devil wins."

Aunt Millie from their church joined them. She greeted everybody. "Koko, we are praying. God will hear us. God is watching over Tiro."

"God is there for white people and not for us," Neo said. "If he were there for us, my brother would not be going to Robben Island." The women shook their heads sadly at Neo's words. She continued. "All the pictures of God's son are white. How could anyone expect a white man to punish white people for tormenting black people? Perhaps our ancestors will punish them."

"Neo," Koko said. "You know better than that. Remember the story of Job?"

"Job was white," Neo said. "Koko, I don't trust God anymore. He favors white people."

"You are almighty, Lord." Koko sang the first line of the hymn. "Never forget the song, Neo."

"You are all powerful," Neo sang the second line.

The women smiled.

Ma-Malamba got up. "Let's pour the tea and serve the people in the living room."

Neo's friend Noli came in. "Noli." Neo smiled.

"Looks like you two have catching up to do," Koko said, "Go play outside, get some fresh air."

People came and went at the Marus until late at night.

After the last guest left, Koko, Evelyn and Neo sat by the fire in the kitchen. Neo yawned.

"Go to bed, Neo," Koko said. "I'll join you later."

Neo shook her head. "I'm not going to bed until Pitso and Kagiso come back."

Evelyn and Koko shook their heads.

After a while there was a knock at the door.

Evelyn walked towards the door. "Who's there?"

"Mummy." Pitso called out.

She opened the door. "Thank God you're here. Your sister wouldn't go to sleep until you came home."

Neo laughed and got up to go to bed. "Good night."

"Don't forget to pray." Koko said.

Koko got up too. "I'm glad you're home. There's too much crime at night these days. Hard to sleep while you're out there."

"Don't worry Koko," Kagiso said. "We don't go far at night. We were at George's house."

"Besides, there's two of us," Pitso said. "No tsotsi would dare touch us."

"They go around in gangs sometimes," Evelyn said. "You have to watch out."

They did not stay up. Everyone went to bed.

Evelyn was glad Edward was sleeping comfortably. The medication was working. She lay awake thinking about their son, wondering if he was sleeping, if he had a blanket to keep him warm. She wondered if he was already on the train to Robben Island. The blankets were heavy on her and yet she felt cold. She said a silent prayer, "God be with my child." Evelyn remembered the judge's statement when he said had it not been for Tiro's young age he would have imposed the death sentence. She continued to pray silently. "Protect him and keep him alive." She thought of her dead father. She knew that even beyond the grave her father would pray for Tiro and God would hear.

Finally she fell asleep.

That night, as Neo lay in bed, she heard something running outside, light footsteps, maybe dogs. She heard something fall, a metallic sound like the lid of a trash can as a dog tipped it over to scrounge for food. She heard a car stop in front of the house. Security Police? She raised her head to listen for the knock. The car drove away. She saw dancing stars in the dark. She heard low conspiratorial voices in the street. She shut her eyes but the stars continued to dance inside her eyes. She drifted in and out of sleep until she couldn't tell the difference anymore. This must be what people experience before they die, she thought. A drifting in and out until their souls drift away at last.

Towards dawn she finally fell asleep. She heard the heavy sound of thunderstorms. Clouds rolled and a thin wind whistled hauntingly. Lightning crisscrossed the dark sky. It got darker.

Then, she heard it—the sound of the army tank. She looked up and it was rolling towards her. She ran away from the tank towards the river. The tank kept coming. She stood at the edge of the river wandering whether to jump in. The water swirled furiously, big waves lashing in all directions. Neo looked, and there amidst the waves was Mamogashwa. Her eyes threw sparks and she lashed her snake-tail up and down and sideways.

Neo wavered precariously on the river bank between the fast-approaching tank and Mamogashwa. But she slipped and fell into the river. She tried to scream, but her voice was trapped in her throat. She flailed about, kicking furiously struggling to stay afloat.

She woke up panting and queasy. When she opened her eyes, she saw dancing stars; and then she sobbed.

The bedside lamp came on.

"Neo," Koko said. "Are you dreaming?"

Neo got out of bed and ran to the bathroom. "I'm going to throw up dirty water."

Koko followed her into the bathroom.

Neo leaned over the toilet bowl and vomited, while Koko rubbed her upper back gently.

"It's all right," Koko said. "Get it all out."

Finally, Neo leaned over the sink and rinsed her mouth.

"Let's go back to sleep," Koko said.

"No." Neo shook her head. "It's daytime." She walked into the hallway and into the kitchen. Koko followed her.

"It's too early *ngwanangwanake*," Koko said.

"No," Neo said. "I don't want to sleep."

"Was it the drowning dream again?" Koko asked.

Neo nodded. "Yes, the one with the army tank, Mamogashwa, the scary noises and the turbulent river. My ears hurt."

"Remember, you have to pray very hard every night and every morning," Koko said. "That will help. God will drive the monsters away. Don't give up."

"I'm tired of praying," Neo said. "It's not helping. Anyway, I don't want to pray to the God of white people."

"No," Koko said. "That is what white people want you to believe. The true God is not the white God. He is the God of all."

"If there was a God," Neo started, "He'd kill all the bad white people and Tiro wouldn't be in Robben Island."

"I'll tell you what to do when next you fall into the river," Koko said. "Look very carefully through the darkness. Look and you'll see a man with his hand outstretched, ready to pull you to safety. That will be your grandfather. Remember him from the pictures?"

"But he's dead."

"Yes," Koko said. "And that is good, because he is now part of your ancestors. He is always around you, and so he can help you anywhere. So, look carefully, and you'll see him at least in silhouette. Keep your eyes glued to him and your souls will connect. Nothing will touch you as long as you're connected. He's always there; just train yourself to look carefully and you will see him."

Neo thought of the framed picture of her maternal grandfather that sat on the side table next to her mother's bed. In it he was squatting among beautiful flowers. Neo was prepared to try.

CHAPTER 16

Liquor Raid

Neo went to the store with her friend Noli. They crossed the tarred road into Section S and passed the police station where a fleet of gray vans were parked. A few yards beyond the police station was a big walled block of yellow brick with no windows—the beer hall where sorghum beer was sold. Only men could enter the hall.

There were rumors the government added secret chemicals to make the men addicted to its beer. Others whispered they even added a compound designed to make black men infertile so as to reduce the number of black men.

Bicycles were parked outside the entrance and young boys guarded them for a small fee. A lot of men in overalls and khaki work clothes entered the place. There was no dress code. The metal double-doors were wide open showing the courtyard where men sat on benches and drank from two-pint and quart brown plastic beakers.

The smell of sorghum beer filled the air.

"Want to hear the beer-hall joke?" Neo asked.

"Yes," Noli said.

"One day a little boy walked to the store with his mother and when they passed here he said to his mother, 'Ma, this place smells like Daddy,' and the mother said 'that's because he's in there right now.'"

Noli laughed. "Yes, their breath is bad when they've had sorghum beer."

It was Friday afternoon—payday. A few women hung outside the beer hall and waited for their husbands, laborers who were paid with cash, to make sure they got some money for their families before it disappeared into the beer hall, or before the men could be robbed by tsotsis later on their way home.

Loud Mbaqanga music, with a fast urgent beat and vibrant urgent rhythms, blared from inside. The penny whistle and guitar sounds fused to produce a pulsating beat that made one want to dance. A municipal policeman in khaki uniform stood at the entrance to the beer hall.

Outside the only public entrance to the beer hall, a line of women sat with big dishes of grilled sweet potatoes, boiled and fried peanuts, with and without their shells, and fried fish bones. Nearby, several homemade braziers, made out of old paraffin drums, burned, heat coming out of the many holes on the sides. The smells, of acidic smoldering coal, aromatic cinnamon sweet potatoes, oily fish bones, smoky grilled meat, sour sorghum beer, and dust mixed to produce a heady aroma.

Near the women, a man in blue overalls sold offal and liver out of his bicycle carrier. He squeezed a rubber bell to attract customers.

"*Mogodu sebete mogodu sebete*," he shouted as he waved the buzzing flies away with a piece of newspaper.

One of the women said, "Ai! popopopo is making noise with his tube thing." She imitated the flat sound of the tube.

Smoke hovered around.

A small barefoot boy with a bulky tattered v-neck green sweater held the sides of a big box of oranges hanging around his small neck. "Oranges, oranges, two for tickey two for tickey," the boy called.

A man in a black fedora hat sold pants, shirts and socks out of the open trunk of his black Chevrolet car.

On the wall outside the beer hall, posters advertised "Castle Beer, the beer of the distinctive man," with a young man wearing a suit and tie, and "Ashbury Gin, the man's liquor," with an older man in blue suit and tie.

Neo and Noli walked past the cinema and crossed the street to a row of shops. On the corner was the cafe which belonged to Mr. Phiri, who also owned the cinema. Next to the cafe was a dairy, then a butcher, then a general store owned by Mr. Kgotso, a family friend.

Neo and Noli walked into the store, bought bleach and left, taking the long way home.

The community hall was across the street from a string of businesses that included Doctor Moleti's surgery, a small tailor shop, and a funeral home.

"There's Beki's uncle," Noli said. He passed them.

"His lips are burned," Neo said. "They are pink."

"Mampuru lips," Noli said, meaning red lips burnt by Mampuru the potent home brew.

Not far from their street, they saw police vans and municipal police surrounding Ma-Malamba's house. The house was a shebeen, a private house where liquor was sold, illegally. A few years earlier the government had passed a law prohibiting the selling of liquuor in a private home. Brewing and selling traditional sorghum beer was also illegal. Shebeens were popular. The government didn't want this competition as shebeens took business away from the government's own beerhalls.

They ran to see what was happening. A crowd formed quickly. Neo and Noli held hands and worked their way to the front, squeezing past people. The police banged on the tin door which made a loud metallic boom.

"Open, woman, open!" the policeman shouted and kicked the door. "We'll break this door!"

There was no response.

"Open! Oopen!," the police shouted again.

"Go away," Ma-Malamba shouted from inside the house.

Suddenly, out of a window, rusty mampuru splashed to the ground. It smelled like fermented sour pineapple. People clapped, cheered and laughed.

Neo knew every mampuru maker had some secret potions. They differed from woman to woman and the secret wasn't revealed to thwart competition. Ma-Malamba's Mampuru was popular. On weekends, crowds of men filled her living room and kitchen. They stood on the verandah in the front of the house, on wooden back-less benches under the peach trees.

"We'll break the door, woman!" the stocky policeman shouted.

She finally opened the door and two policemen grabbed her, dragging her into the yard.

"Leave me alone. I have no beer. I only had the little bit that I made for my husband."

"It's Mampuru. Its illegal to make it, even if you aren't selling," the policeman said. "You come in, woman. You can tell your lies to the judge."

"It's not Mampuru. it's regular sorghum beer. I just threw in some pineapple because my husband likes pineapple. It's not Mampuru!"

A woman shouted, "They don't have time for the criminals! But they have time to go around bothering women who make beer for their husbands in their own home."

"These dogs!" another woman shouted.

Neo and Noli pushed their way towards the front of the house where the police van was parked. The police threw Ma-Malamba in the back and slammed the door shut. Through the wire mesh they could see Ma-Malamba's silhouette. The van sped off leaving a cloud of dust behind it. Children scrambled to get out of the way.

On their way home Neo and Noli walked behind a group of women.

"Serves her right," a woman with a green head scarf said. "She's killing women's husbands with her Mampuru."

"I hope they keep her there for good," said the woman with a blue wool knitted hat pulled over her ears.

"You know her, how she does favors," the woman with the scarf said. "She'll be back before you know it."

"It's a pity," the one with the blue hat said. "They take our husband's money. They should be locked away for good."

"The only reason they arrest her now is because that fat sergeant no longer comes there," the one with the green scarf said.

"She takes men's money with the beer and when they are drunk, she searches them and steals the rest," a woman said. "She doesn't care that their children go hungry."

"Look at MaSinah," the one with a green scarf said, "Poor woman. The man goes there after work before he goes home, everyday. But, she can't say anything because he beats her up."

"I'm surprised they raided her," one woman said. "Considering how many police drink there."

Despite constant harassment by the police, shebeens persisted, survived, even flourished, because they were more convenient than the cold formal government beer halls. Women could come too.

Neo and Noli went home.

CHAPTER 17

Survival

When Neo returned from the store, she found her mother in the kitchen stirring a pot of soup.

"The police raided Ma-Malamba's house," Neo said.

"What?" Evelyn said. "What kind of police?"

"The liquor ones," Neo said.

"Oh. That's probably just a fine. She'll be out."

"Yes," Neo said. "It's just a fine for liquor, right?"

"Yes," Evelyn said. "Usually two months in jail, or a fine. So she'll be out tomorrow morning. They are silly. They arrest women who are just trying to make a living in these tough times. They need to go after criminals who assault people."

"She's going to sleep in prison?" Neo asked.

"Not to worry," Evelyn said. "She'll be out tomorrow morning as soon as she appears before the magistrate."

"I'm going to sleep at Koko's house," Neo said. "I'll go now before it gets dark."

"How about tomorrow?" Evelyn asked. "Let's go into the living room. They are waiting for us. We need to talk."

Neo felt a knot in her stomach. Talks were likely to be about problems.

In the living room, Edward sat on a chair. Next to him, Pitso bent over a suitcase. Kagiso sat cross-legged on the floor.

Neo announced, "The liquor squad arrested Ma-Malamba."

"The dogs," Pitso said. "Liquor raid again? They are looking for bribes."

"Come in and sit down," Edward said.

Neo squeezed on the rust couch between Edward and Evelyn. In the middle of the room, where the teak table usually sat was a brown suitcase. Neo looked at the suitcase and then at everyone.

"Who's leaving?" Neo said.

"Pitso," her father said.

Neo was relieved it was not her father.

"By the way, you can take your favorite records," Edward said looking at Pitso.

"I've already packed the 'Good Night Dear Lord' Johnny Mathis recor," Pitso said.

"Take whatever you want," Evelyn said. "Take. We can always replace them."

Pitso knelt before the record rack. He opened the suitcase on the floor and placed several records on top.

"My dear, it's getting late," Evelyn said.

Edward cleared his throat.

"*Banake*," he said. "Your brother is leaving tonight, leaving the country."

Neo's eyes felt hot, but she forced a slight smile. Her cheeks were taut.

"We thought it best he leave, just to be on the safe side so he doesn't also end up in prison," Edward said. "This morning the Special Branch picked him up in the street and kept him for three hours. They let him go, but he might not be so lucky next time."

Neo clasped her hands tightly. Evelyn cleared her throat.

Edward took off his glasses, and brushed his eyes with his hands. "It is best he leave immediately. Nobody knows who is going to be arrested next."

Neo fixed her gaze on Edward's pipe in the stone ashtray on the edge of the table. It looked lonely. The room was quiet for a moment.

Evelyn squeezed Neo's shoulder. "Botswana is near, it's not too far."

Neo nodded and attempted a tight smile. She wanted to give the impression that she was taking this lightly.

"He's not going to get lost there," Edward said. "He will stay with Puo."

Evelyn stood and pushed her hair back with both hands. "Double-check to make sure you have everything," she said.

Pitso looked into his suitcase and then closed it. "All set." He stood, adjusted his pants and put on his brown jacket. They all rose and came together in a circle.

Pitso shook hands with Kagiso. They looked at each other, then hugged tightly.

Next Pitso hugged Neo. "I'm going to miss you, but I'm going to see you soon."

Tears streamed down Neo's face. She tried to smile through the tears. It was like the bit of rain that falls from a stray cloud while the sun shines all around.

Edward hugged Pitso. "Look after yourself son."

"Mummy." Pitso hugged her.

"Everything is going to work out," Evelyn said and smiled.

Edward and Kagiso drove Pitso to the station.

"Let's go heat the soup." Evelyn and Neo went into the kitchen.

"Do you know how they test to see if someone is crazy at the hospital where Noli's mother works?" Neo asked.

"No, how?"

"They make them fill a bottomless drum with water, a big paraffin drum, and if they keep pouring water and can't realize the drum is hollow, then they are mad."

Evelyn laughed. "Neo, where do you get all this?"

Neo laughed too. But then she suddenly became solemn. "Is Tiro already in Robben Island?"

"Probably," Evelyn said.

"How are they getting there?" she asked. "In police vans?"

"Maybe by train," Evelyn said. "We don't know for sure."

"When can we visit him?" Neo asked.

"Well," Evelyn said. "We can't see him for the first three months."

"Three months." Neo silently calculated in her head. "Good. We can go during the Christmas vacation. I'll be home then."

"Actually," Evelyn said slowly. "They don't allow people under sixteen to visit Robben Island."

"So, I won't see him for three years!" Neo cried.

"Three years will pass quickly, you'll see."

"I'll write to him a lot then," Neo said.

"We'll have to coordinate that," Evelyn said. "Because he'll be allowed only one letter a month."

"One?" Neo said.

Evelyn held both Neo's hands in her own. "Things will get better with time." Evelyn's mouth was pursed and her forehead had deep wrinkles.

Kagiso and Edward returned and they all had soup and bread in the dining room.

When they were done with soup Evelyn brought a bowl of black grapes.

"These are huge, Mummy," Neo said.

Evelyn nodded. "Yes."

Neo rolled a grape between her fingers. "It says on the box they are from the Cape."

"You're right, Neo," Edward said. "These are from the Cape. They have the best grapes."

Neo put the grape in the palm of her right hand and rolled it slowly with the index finger her left hand. "Maybe they have a lot of grapes on Robben Island and Tiro will have some."

Kagiso changed the subject. "I'm tired today. I think I'll go to bed early." He got up and started clearing the table. "Neo, will you help me do the dishes?"

Neo got up and helped him.

They all went to bed early.

In bed that night, the night of Pitso's departure, Neo lay on her back awake, thinking about Pitso and Tiro. She saw Tiro squished in a police van on bumpy roads. He sat bent over, in a train compartment shackled to the door, the train swaying roughly from side to side and the metal wheels clanging and banging all around him. There was no one to comfort him.

She imagined Pitso on a long dirt road by himself, carrying a suitcase.

Home was never going to be the same and she would never be happy again. The pain would always be intense. How was she going to live like this? All these empty spaces left by Pitso and Tiro made her home eerie like a place about to be demolished, like a neighborhood where some homes were already destroyed and a few were still standing. How long would it be before they came for her father and Kagiso? There seemed to be a curse on her family.

Tears flowed down the sides of her face into her ears. When she heard the knock on the door she blew her nose and wiped the tears quickly.

"Neo, can I come in for a minute?" Evelyn whispered.

"Come in." she sniffed.

"Saw your light on," Evelyn said. "Just want to see if you need anything."

"No, I'm sleepy," she said and affected a yawn. She turned to face the wall. Tears streamed onto the pillow.

"Brought you an extra blanket," Mummy said. "They forecast a very cold night." She covered Neo. "If you get up before me tomorrow, wake me up."

Neo pulled the blanket over her head. "Goodnight," she said softly.

Evelyn stroked Neo's head through the blankets. "I know it's very hard for you now, but things are going to get better." Evelyn kissed Neo on the head. "Good night. Should I turn off the light?"

"No," Neo said.

Even after Evelyn left the room, Neo did not pray. She was angry with God. All the praying she'd done did not help her brother. So what was the use?

When she finally fell asleep, the army tank rolled towards her. She could not get up to run. The mechanical monster rolled over her. She screamed and woke up. She sat on the bed and leaned against the headboard. She stayed that way, sleeping sitting up, waking every time she tipped over. Then she'd readjust and doze off again. She knew in that position the army tank couldn't get her.

CHAPTER 18

Freedom Run

The one thing Evelyn hated about winter was the fact that the sun set so quickly and there wasn't enough time to work outside. It was only seven and she, Edward, and Neo were already inside, huddled around the stove.

"I think I'm beating this flu," Edward said. "I'm not so congested anymore."

Evelyn said, "You have to be careful though."

"My whole body is tired from sleeping, so much," Edward said.

There was a knock and Evelyn opened the door.

"Mother," Evelyn said, "so late at night. You aren't afraid of tsotsis?"

"It's not so late," Koko said. "it just gets dark so early."

"It's not safe these days," Edward said. "Especially for women."

"Anything the matter?" Evelyn asked. "You look subdued."

Koko blew her dry nose.

"Kagiso and George were at my house a while ago," Koko said. "They're leaving the country."

"Leaving the country?" Evelyn screamed. "Oh God! Are they in trouble? What happened?"

"Security police, in two cars, were at George's house," Koko began, "and they, apparently, were anxious to find out where George was. They searched the house top to bottom and took some papers. The lead policeman said they'd be back another time because they wanted to ask him some questions. Kagiso and George said they heard the police were very anxious so it looks like there's some trouble."

"Oh, my God,!" Evelyn exclaimed. "What is this? They are just going to arrest all our children?"

"They are the rulers," Koko said. "They're like Herod, they think they are God."

"So what happened?" Edward asked.

"They say they decided to run because they'd heard there was a crack-down and this confirms it. George took some clothes, and they decided not to come here for Kagiso's clothes in case the police came here. They said they'll share George's clothes."

"What's going on? Edward asked. "God. My children. Did they say where they were going to hide?"

"Botswana," Koko said.

"That's good," Edward said "I'll arrange to send their clothes over. Kagiso knows Puo's house in Kanye. It's far from the capital and therefore safer. They'll be comfortable there. They can join Pitso."

Edward was referring to Puo, who lived with them as a young man while going through High School and teacher training in the forties. He and Evelyn helped him through teacher-training. He was an orphan and always regarded the Marus as family. He was a good model brother for the boys.

"Will they be able to run away from the police?" Neo shook Edward's shoulder. "Ntate, Ntate. Are they in trouble? Are they going to be arrested? Tell me. Tell me." Neo spoke so fast she was out of breath.

"Neo," Evelyn said. "Calm down. You have to be quiet now. We are not sure ourselves. We have to take care of things."

"We'll explain things to you later my child." Edward took Neo's hand.

Neo sobbed.

Edward turned to Koko. "What about money? Did they borrow somewhere?"

"I gave them all the money I had in the house," Koko said.

"I'll go to the bank tomorrow," Edward said. "Thank you, Koko. How much was it?"

"No, no. They are my children too," Koko said.

Evelyn felt lucky, her mother always kept money at home, a habit stemming from the old days when they did not trust banks.

Evelyn said. "We are going to give you the money back."

"To do what with it?" Koko asked. "Let's just thank God the children are going to be safe. "

Edward changed the subject. "I thank God for giving them the sense to realize they shouldn't come here. The police must be watching the house."

Evelyn turned to her mother. "We did not want to alarm you, but there's a strange white car that slows down when it passes our house. And the other day, two men came here looking for Pitso, claiming to be his friends. I could feel it. They were police informers."

"Mummy, what men," Neo shouted. "When did the men come? You didn't tell me. What did they want?"

"It was nothing important," Evelyn said slowly, trying to sound casual. "So we forgot about it."

Neo trurned to Koko. "Koko, I'm scared. I hear sounds at night."

"Don't worry," Koko said. "It's been windy the past few nights. Don't forget prayer drives all fears away." She hugged Neo and kissed her on the head. "I'll see you tomorrow." Koko said.

Neo wished Koko were staying the night, but she did not say anything.

That night Neo kept the light on in her room. She slept very little, in fits and starts making it difficult for the night-mares to develop fully.

Later, Evelyn and Edward stayed awake talking for most of the night.

"It looks like there's a crackdown going on," Evelyn said.

"I'm glad Kagiso remembered the talk we had," Edward said. "When I told him that if he ever suspected that he was in trouble, to escape to Botswana."

"I wish Tiro had skipped," Evelyn said sadly.

"I don't understand all this." Edward shook his head. "I thought I knew my children. I thought I'd know if they were doing political things."

"They take vows of secrecy in the Movement," Evelyn said.

Edward was silent. They lay side by side, staring all night at the enormous blank ceiling, feeling too numb to hope. Both of them did not sleep much that night.

CHAPTER 19

Township Politics

The sun was struggling to come up, but Evelyn was already working in the garden in front. Andrew, a young man from a few streets down, greeted her. Evelyn liked him. She had taught him many years ago. He was a good student, and well-behaved child.

Andrew came closer. "Mistress have you heard"

"Heard what?"

"They burned down Peter's house," Andrew said. "Being a Special Branch fellow, you know the Security Police are going to search to find the killer. A lot of innocent people are going to get beaten up. I hope whoever did it is out of the country now. After what he did to his own cousin-"

"Wait," Evelyn said. "What are you talking about?"

"We heard commotion last night around two a.m. and we rushed out."

Evelyn was shaking with impatience. "What happened? What?"

"The Noga mansion, as he liked to call it, is burned down."

"My God."

Andrew continued. "He was shot dead, but his wife and children were not hurt, I hear. They were taken away before we got there, by the police."

Evelyn could not believe it. "Are they sure Peter is dead?"

She did not feel sorry, but she made sure to restrain herself. She was still angry about Peter's role in Tiro's trial.

Andrew turned to walk away. "I'm sorry, Mistress, have to go. Can't miss my train."

"Oh, yes, sorry to delay you," Evelyn said. "Thank you for the news. Actually, I shouldn't say 'thank you.' You know what they say-we should not say thanks for bad news."

As she watched Andrew walk away, Evelyn felt a chill. It's not that she felt sorry for Peter. He got what he deserved. But she was concerned. Did Kagiso have anything to do with it? How was she going to tell her husband?

Finally she stood and ran to their bedroom where Edward slept.

"Edward," she said, as soon as she opened the door. She did not wait for him to answer. "They say Peter's dead."

"Peter?" Edward sat up quickly, his feet pressed to the floor.

"His house was burned down." Evelyn spoke fast, as if she couldn't wait to get out all the words. "And the car too. Peter was shot."

"Do they know who did it?"

Evelyn shook her head. "Andrew says the police are not talking."

"Where are the children? Where's poor Rose?" Edward asked.

"The police took them away. Apparently they're safe."

Edward got up. "I have to go to them."

"No, you can't go out in this cold morning air." Evelyn said. "The last thing we need is for you to get pneumonia. I have more than enough problems as it is."

"I have to see about the children. I'm not so congested anymore."

"They are not even there," Evelyn said. "The police took them."

"Evelyn, we'll have to find them and help them. The children are innocent."

"I'm not sure I trust Rose anymore either." Evelyn said. "If she didn't agree with what he was doing, why didn't she come here like everybody else after my child was sent to prison?"

"Put yourself in her shoes," Edward said. "You know she must have been scared. She must have been afraid, or ashamed, even though she's innocent."

"Afraid of what?" Evelyn asked. "She had nothing to fear. And, yes, I'd like to be in her shoes. With all my children home, not strewn all over the place. Even when I eat, I can't enjoy my food because I don't know if my children have anything to eat!

"Please keep your voice low, my dear, please," Edward said.

"Sorry." Evelyn began straightening the blankets.

Edward said, "Peter has hurt this family deeply, but we can't wipe out the fact that his mother is our sister, and his wife, poor thing, is innocent too."

"Your sister, not mine." Evelyn said. "I thank God I don't have a sister. Who knows? Maybe her children would be selling my children to the dogs."

Edward sighed deeply. "We have to try to find someone to go to Fafung to tell my mother and Mary."

Evelyn did not respond. They both sat on the bed and kept quiet for a while.

After what seemed like a long time to Evelyn, Edward broke the silence. "I'm worried about something. Do you think-"

"I know what you are thinking," Evelyn said.

"Can't be." Edward shook his head, "Kagiso wouldn't be involved in this. Pitso, yes. If he were around, I would have suspected him immediately."

"I thought about that too," Evelyn said. "Kagiso and George left so quickly last night. They must have left for the border immediately."

"We have to go see what happened," Edward said.

"No, my dear. The morning air is not good for your cold. The children are not there. You can go see the house later when the air has warmed up. I'll go see."

Evelyn ran out.

People were crowded around what was left of Peter's house. It was a brick shell. The beautiful bricks were now black, full of soot. Windows were broken. The big rose brush under the living room window was burned, and Evelyn thought it was a shame. It used to produce big beautiful yellow roses.

Evelyn approached a policeman guarding the house. "What happened?

"Well," he said. "We know for sure Peter's dead. The wife and kids were taken to safety, but we don't know where."

"My husband is his uncle," Evelyn said.

The policeman smiled, and extended his hand to greet Evelyn. "Yes, I know, Mistress. You taught my brother." He paused. "I don't know anything, Mistress. We are just in the criminal division. It's the security division that handles these matters. They don't trust us. They are right. We hate this arbitrary arrest business of innocent people who have not committed real crimes. Saying you hate this government should not be a crime. These Security people tarnish the image of the whole police force."

Evelyn was surprised by the man's openness. It was clear he did not like the Security Police. "Don't worry. People know the difference."

"We heard about your son's sentence, and Peter's role," he said. "It must be hard for you."

"It hurts to be betrayed by a blood relative." Evelyn said.

One of the women came closer to listen to Evelyn and the policeman and another policeman told her to stand back.

Evelyn thanked the policeman and left.

A woman tried to talk to her, but Evelyn rushed away. Her mind was running in all directions.

At home, Evelyn found Edward sitting at the kitchen table. He supported his jaw with one hand, and poured sugar into his cup with the other. Evelyn stood, watching him pour one teaspoon after another.

"So many spoons, my dear," she finally said.

Edward was startled. "You're back. I didn't hear you come in." He sneezed.

Evelyn poured Edward a fresh cup of tea.

Edward rubbed the sides of his nose between the eyes where the eye-glasses anchored, and then squeezed his eyes. He shook his head from side to side gently.

Evelyn told him what she'd seen and heard.

"My poor sister," Edward said. "Imagine, she's lost her only child, after raising him by herself. I can't understand why Peter involved himself in such despicable nonsense. It's not as though he was starving."

"Greed," Evelyn said. "You know he's always been a bit greedy. Always living way above his means."

"But this?"

"It's bad enough being a sell-out," Evelyn said. "But sell his own cousin, after all we've done for him. But I guess someone who cannot even take care of his own mother, really, wouldn't find it difficult to sell anybody."

"You know," Edward said. "His father's abandonment really affected him. Made him bitter, and insecure. That explains his lack of loyalty."

"Ah, my dear," Evelyn said. "You're always ready to make psychological excuses for everybody. He was not a child."

"There are many people who are spies," Edward said.

Evelyn said, "I think we have to find out where his children are and help them and we have to go notify his mother. I feel sorry for Mary."

They sat in front of the stove, open in front, and watched the sparks fly.

Neo entered the kitchen. She rubbed her eyes. "Morning," she said.

"Morning my child." Edward said.

Evelyn forced a smile. "Good, you slept very well today,"

"I fell asleep at dawn," Neo said. She looked at Edward. "How come Ntate's cold takes so long to heal? His eyes look red."

Edward smiled. "I feel better my child. Sit here next to me." He felt comforted by Neo's presence.

Evelyn looked at Edward and then at Neo. "Neo, get the box of tissues from my dressing table."

As soon as Neo left the room, Evelyn whispered to Edward. "Let's not tell her now. Let's wait until later when she's fully awake."

Neo returned with the tissues and sat next to them.

They both smiled.

CHAPTER 20

The News

The one o'clock news started with an urgent report.

A somber male voice reported, "Five young black South African men were shot and killed in a house in Gaberone, Botswana. Informed sources suggest that they were part of a group of communist terrorists who had been trained to infiltrate South Africa. The house in which they were staying is a known half-way house for communist terrorists on the way to South Africa to carry out terrorist attacks. Sources suspect the attack to be part of internal struggles within the communist movements."

"Oh my God," Evelyn said. "Thank God we have Puo in Kanye. Otherwise, Pitso and Kagiso would be in Gaberone. It's the Security Police as usual, killing people who have fled to other countries. I don't know who they think they are fooling."

"Yes, we are lucky to have Puo in Botswana," Edward said. "He can guide them, and they don't have to be stranded there."

"I emphasized to Pitso that he should go straight to Puo's and not hang around the capital," Evelyn said, "Gaberone is not safe anymore. It's just like being in South Africa. Those murders are obviously the work of South African forces."

"Life is just a chance," Edward said. "one never knows."

That evening, a young black man came to their house. Evelyn was in the kitchen. His eyes darted around and Evelyn was suspicious. Another one of the Security Police traps? This one is not even smooth. Evelyn was irritated but she softened up when the young man took off his hat and extended his hand respectfully.

"Good evening, Mistress. Mistress Maru?" the young man said.

"I'm Philip Nkosi" he said. "This Pitso and Kagiso's home?"

Evelyn pulled a chair out. "Yes, please sit down."

Philip fidgeted with his cap. "I'm in the same movement with Pitso."

"Mmm," Evelyn responded. She noticed the young man sat on the edge of the chair as though ready to run at the slightest sign of trouble.

"Er. I'm sorry, Mistress, I have bad news," Philip said. "Pitso and Kagiso were killed in the shooting in Gaberone."

Evelyn pushed away her chair and got up. "Both of them?" Evelyn screamed. "Are you sure? How do you know?"

"I'm sorry," the young man said. "We are absolutely sure. I've been sent by the Movement. I also have to let you know that the Movement will pay all your traveling expenses and so on. Of course, they'll take care of all the funeral expenses in Botswana. Since they left without passports, those bastards will not allow you to bury them here at home."

Evelyn dry-wiped her face with her hands and went to the window by the sink and looked out.

"I'm sorry," Philip said.

"Let me get their father," Evelyn said. "So he can hear this for himself."

The young man got up abruptly. "I have to leave. Your house is probably being watched. I hope to see you in Botswana, I'll be crossing tonight. They are looking for me."

"Was one of the boys who died George Malamba?" Evelyn asked.

"No."

"Thank God," Evelyn said. "I'd hate to have to tell his mother. Are you sure?"

"Very sure."

He left, and quickly disappeared into the night. Evelyn stood there wondering if all this was just a nightmare. She collected herself and went to the bedroom to tell her husband.

She sat on the bed next to him. "My dear," Evelyn said. "Pitso and Kagiso have been killed. That radio report yesterday…"

Edward did not get up. He lay on his back and tears streamed freely down the sides of his face. Some went into his ears. He did not attempt to wipe them.

Evelyn's tears stung like acid clouding her eyes, but they did not drop.

Edward and Evelyn agreed that Evelyn, who still had her passport, should go to Botswana. The following day, Edward would go to his lawyer's office first thing in the morning, and see if he could help him get his passport back from the Security Police.

The door opened and Neo walked in. "I'm sorry I'm late." she said, "I was waiting for these scones to come out of the oven and this bottle here is lemon juice. Koko said it would kill all Ntate's cold germs. He should drink it," Neo said.

Evelyn and Edward looked at each other.

Neo began to shake. "What are you hiding?"

Evelyn said, "Come, sit here, we'll tell you everything."

Neo sat carefully on the edge of the chair as though ready for flight in case the news was dangerous.

"My child," Edward started in his usual deliberate slow way only now it was worse because he was weak. "My child, it's bad news—"

Neo interrupted, tapping the table quickly with her open palm. "Tell me quickly. Mummy, tell me quickly."

"Pitso and Kagiso are dead, Neo," Evelyn said.

Neo jumped and ran to her bedroom. She rolled on the floor screaming, "I want my brothers. I want my brothers."

Evelyn followed her. She almost fell trying to lift Neo off the floor. She took Neo's hand and got her to sit on the bed. She held her while she cried.

The following afternoon, Edward listened to the lawyer tell him he couldn't go to Botswana, not legally that is. "I'm sorry Mr. Maru, it didn't work. We tried everything, it was a long shot but I gave it everything, pleaded and pleaded."

Edward was shocked even though he knew from the beginning that they wouldn't return his passport. The Boers were vindictive and had lost any semblance of humanity.

Weakly, Edward asked, "Why?"

"The man at the Passport Office said it was out of their hands. It was now a Security Police issue and no one could do anything about it. He was actually sympathetic to your case, I was surprised."

Edward stood looking through the window facing West. He wiped his eyes. He pointed, "Botswana is that way. Who will bury my children? My children." He was barely audible. It was as though if he said one more word, all the breath will leave his body and there would be nothing left to keep him alive. He held on to the window frame.

"I'm sorry, Mr. Maru," the lawyer said. "At the Security Police offices they wouldn't even let me see any senior officer. I tried."

Edward turned around. "Thank you very much."

"I'm sorry." the lawyer said again.

Edward could not even remember how he drove home that day. It was a hazy journey, everything in a blur.

CHAPTER 21

Rest

Evelyn was not surprised to find her house full of people when she returned from Botswana. They knew she was returning that day, so naturally, she assumed they'd gathered to welcome her back and offer their condolences. She was exhausted and needed to rest, but then it would've hurt if she'd come back and the house was empty. She thought it was nice that they were there to mourn with her, as was the tradition even though her children's corpses weren't there. Some women cried when she entered the house. Evelyn slumped on a chair and her mother hugged her.

"How was it?" Koko asked. "Everybody was here, and we held the wake the night before the funerals, as though the funeral was here. Everybody from church was here."

"We buried the boys," Evelyn said.

Neo cried and mother and daughter hugged. Neo's body shook and Evelyn held her tight.

"I know it hurts very much now," Evelyn said. "But it is going to be all right."

Koko put her arm around Evelyn.

"Let's go to your bedroom," Koko said. "There are some things we have to discuss immediately."

Neo followed them in.

It was traditional when there was a death for women to sit on the floor in a room in the house, until the burial. Then after the funeral, the women would leave the room, and the furniture returned to its normal place. So Evelyn was surprised to find her bed had not been returned and her women friends and relatives sat on the mattress on the floor. She thought maybe they waited for her before leaving the room so she could see that they fulfilled their role and supported her.

"Thank you," Evelyn said. "We buried them. It's all done. We can begin picking up the pieces of our lives."

"Sit down here," Koko said.

The sobbing continued. Evelyn was the only one whose tears were not falling.

Koko cleared her throat. "Ma-Pitso," Koko said, "there is some bad news."

Before Koko could continue, Evelyn said, "It's all bad news these days. They will not stop until they've finished all our children."

"Edward died yesterday," Koko said. "A heart attack."

Evelyn didn't speak immediately. She looked directly at her mother.

The room was completely silent now, no sobbing. It was a strained pause, like the very brief silence after a child's wild scream.

"My God," Evelyn finally said.

At her words, the women cried. Some sobbed loudly. Evelyn was numb.

Evelyn began making the funeral arrangements for her husband without actually thinking about Edward. She had hardened into a block of steel. It was the only way she could survive.

The community buried Edward. Everybody said it was the biggest funeral Melodi had ever seen. It was actually a funeral for Pitso and Kagiso as well. Crowds of students from Hebron and other high schools arrived in school uniform. Many of them defiantly wore yellow and green ribbons representing the colors of the Movement. Some defiantly held the Movement's flag, which was illegal. Even though Edward hadn't been politically active, his funeral was a political funeral.

There was no rest for Evelyn. Two days after the funeral, school opened. Her principal supported her request for a week's leave, and actually insisted she take two weeks off. Neo would also be late for school.

Evelyn and Koko discussed Neo's situation.

"Now, I want her to go back." Evelyn said. "I don't want her to be around. She'll be better off at Moroka with other kids-away from all these troubles. The routines and structures of boarding school will help her."

"I think so too," Koko said. "But convincing her, will be another matter. We have to convince her to do it willingly and not force her."

"I'm afraid that no matter what she thinks I'm going to have to insist," Evelyn said. "We know it's best for her. The one person who would convince her is gone. I don't know how my child is going to survive her father's death."

Thunder roared outside, loud deep thunder.

Evelyn said, "The earth is soaked. We are all going to be wading in mud. The foundations of our homes will not hold. The houses will be stuck in mud and it'll take us a long time to dig out."

Thunder roared again as though to confirm what she was saying.

The sky settled and the rain must have changed direction because it started beating softly on the window.

Neo came into the room and sat next to Koko.

Koko touched her hand. "You are such a wonderful girl, Neo."

Neo pulled her hand. "I don't want to go back, Koko," Neo said, through the tears.

They tried to reason with Neo, but she stood firm.

"Neo," Evelyn said. "You know that's what your father would have wished."

Neo looked up at her mother and stopped crying.

"I'll go," Neo said.

"Know what?" Evelyn said, "You will come home for Easter, for the September short break, and all other long-weekends. You won't have to stay at school like before. We'll send someone to pick you up by car every holiday week-end." Evelyn paused and then continued. "The storm has calmed down. This is good soft rain"

Koko said, "Rain is luck."

"I like this type too," Neo said and looked at her grand-mother. "You know they say Mamogashwa can't travel out of her river hole when there's no storms and tornadoes to wrap herself in."

Koko laughed. "You know what? Our prayers defeated her. She's finally drowned."

Koko came to live with her daughter, Evelyn. She was her only daughter, and that was where she was going to end up anyway and this was as good a time as any to move in. This made Neo very happy.

Epilogue

Later Neo ended up spending many years in Britain working as a lawyer and doing a lot of work for the Movement. She was one of the first to come back in 1990 when her brother Tiro and others were released from Robben Island prison and the Movement was unbanned. She was shocked when she went to visit her old Melodi to find that the river in which Mamogashwa lived was no longer there. It had dried up. She smiled to herself when she recalled how Mamogashwa dreams tormented her when she was a child. She laughed when her childhood friends told journalists that Neo had always been fearless. She usually replied that her brother Tiro, and others like him were the true heroes. They were the ones who risked their lives and freedom, sacrificed their youth to the struggle for freedom.

In 1994, the day before the ceremony when she was sworn in as Minister of Justice Neo took her mother, who was still as energetic as ever, to visit Ntate and Koko's graves. She knelt at the graves. Silently, Neo said to each of them:

"Thank you. I know you always watched and protected me, I'm lucky to have you among my ancestors." She laid yellow and red flowers on the graves. It started drizzling as they left Koko's grave.

"Rain is a sign of luck," Neo said.

Evelyn smiled. "It's a gift, a blessing."

Thunder rumbled deeply, the sound died off slowly, and then fizzled into a murmur. A deep quiet enveloped the earth. Neo and Mummy were accompanied by a soft warm drizzling rain, the kind that nurtures the earth.

Printed in the United States
3997

9 780595 004331